BAD BOYFRIEND

BILLIONAIRE'S CLUB #7

ELISE FABER

BAD BOYFRIEND
BY ELISE FABER
Newsletter sign-up

This is a work of fiction. Names, places, characters, and events are fictitious in every regard. Any similarities to actual events and persons, living or dead, are purely coincidental. Any trademarks, service marks, product names, or named features are assumed to be the property of their respective owners, and are used only for reference. There is no implied endorsement if any of these terms are used. Except for review purposes, the reproduction of this book in whole or part, electronically or mechanically, constitutes a copyright violation.

BILLIONAIRE'S CLUB

Bad Night Stand

Bad Breakup

Bad Husband

Bad Hookup

Bad Divorce

Bad Fiancé

Bad Boyfriend

Bad Blind Date

PROLOGUE

COLLEGE HAD BEEN an utter waste of time.

Though part of that was probably due to the fact that she was graduating with her Master's when her peers were snagging their high school diplomas.

She wasn't bragging. She was just really smart.

College courses at twelve. Bachelor's (with a double major in Mathematics and Computer Science) at sixteen. M.S. in Engineering by eighteen.

And . . . she'd never been kissed.

Never gone on a date.

Which was great news, according to her overprotective father, who wanted to pretend she would be his little girl forever. Not so great when she had the social life of a leaf. A fallen leaf, dried out and crunched underfoot in the middle of winter when all the other leaves had gone to the movies and prom and lost their virginity in the back of Tommy Peddlenton's car.

She digressed, but that was Kelsey. Her mind going in a

million different directions at once, even as she did something completely different with her hands.

Brilliant had been a description of her more than once, and again that wasn't bragging, that was merely how her teachers had always described her. It was why she'd been offered an outrageous sum of money to work for the government beginning in a few weeks, and also why she'd turned down a dozen other offers from the private sector. But her big ole juicy brain—she had her older brother Devon to thank for that lovely description —was also a big reason she was lonely.

She'd been untouchable, undateable. Yes, as complete and utter jailbait until her eighteenth birthday just the month before, she understood exactly why that was. She was glad for it, glad the men she'd gone to school with had treated her with respect and consideration and . . . fine, also like she was asexual.

So *that* part she wasn't exactly grateful for. The rest of it, for sure she was.

Sighing, she fixed her gown, adjusted the colored stole that signified her exit from graduate school, and strode out of her room. Most of her family was downstairs, all wearing proud smiles, even her brother Sebastian, who tended toward quiet and closed down and definitely not verbose with his praise pulled her into a hug and murmured, "Proud of you, Kels."

"Thanks," she murmured back.

"Devon is going to try to make it for the party, sweetheart," her mother said in her softly musical voice. "His plane was delayed, but he's going to get here as soon as he can."

"Okay," she said and meant it. Dev was a professional hockey player, and his team was knee-deep in the playoffs. The fact that he had left, that his coach had allowed it, meant more to her than him seeing her walk across a stage. "Warn him, he owes me extra hugs when he gets here."

Her mom's lips twitched. "I'll do that."

Dev gave the best hugs ever. Probably because he was a giant, and so being hugged by him felt like being enfolded against the chest of a very large teddy bear, but his hugs were also good because he didn't let go. Didn't treat hugging like cursory contact—a wrap and release. He held on like he meant it, and . . . it was impossible not to feel like the most precious object in the universe when she was in his arms.

More digression.

"You know," her dad said, holding out his arms. "I taught him to hug."

Her mom's eyes sparkled. "I'd like to think *I* had something to do with his hugging ability."

"Nope," her dad said. "He got his slapshot from you. His hugs are all mine."

Kels laughed.

Sebastian grinned.

Her mom made an affronted noise and reached for her, but no sooner had her mom's arms closed tight than Kelsey found herself tugged out of the embrace and against her dad's chest. She giggled, then she was tugged away again, but this time into Sebastian's arms. He rivaled Dev in the hugging department, and she was enjoying the contact, the attention, when she was tugged away once more.

She let herself slide free, went willingly, assumed it was her dad claiming her again.

If she'd known who was reaching for her, she never would have allowed the contact. But she'd had her eyes closed, was soaking up her brother laughing and joking and being so fun and loose, a rarity compared with Sebastian's normal demeanor, and so she wasn't paying attention to who'd snagged her.

Wasn't paying attention until she found herself smack nose-first into a chest that was hard and broad, but definitely *not* comforting. Spice and male assaulted her nostrils, and she went from laughing to quiet, every cell in her body standing at attention.

She knew that scent.

Oh shit, she *knew* that scent.

She'd stolen his sweatshirt because of it and wore it to bed every night, no matter how hot it was outside. The smell, the feel, the image of it covering all of Tanner's hard muscles never failed to have heat coiling through her limbs, soaking deep into her abdomen.

Quite simply, that scent made her want.

And the object of her want was currently holding her tightly against his chest, hands running up and down her spine.

He glanced down at her, one half of his mouth curved up. "What do you think, Kels?" Was it her imagination or was there a trace of heat in his expression?

"About what?" she whispered.

"Do I give good hugs?" He tugged her a little closer.

She rubbed her nose across the half-circle of skin exposed above the collar of his sweater, inhaled deeply, trying to absorb his scent into her pores. His breath caught and she leaned back, definitely not missing the heat in his eyes this time.

"Yes," she murmured. "You give good hugs."

His lips curved, his smile hitting her in the gut like a punch.

But it was a good punch.

Because that was the moment Kelsey Scott fell in love.

She'd been crushing hard on Sebastian's friend for years, though he'd never shown her the least bit of interest—other than acting like another brother who was there to tease and annoy and steal her Pringles.

That hug had changed her. Changed *them*.

She'd catapulted over the edge from mere infatuation to offering her heart on a platter when Tanner's arms wrapped around her.

Love. Heady, intoxicating first love.

But feelings aside, that was also the moment she promised herself she was going to get Tanner to hug her again, only the next time, neither of them would be wearing any clothes.

She grinned and stepped away, knowing this was just the beginning.

In some ways, she was right.

She got another hug that night—in fact, many more hugs in the weeks and months that followed—and some of them were of the naked variety.

Unfortunately, she was also very wrong. That moment wasn't a beginning.

It was an end.

And it wasn't first love, heady or intoxicating or otherwise.

It was first hate.

She hated Tanner Pearson with a passion.

ONE

SHE OPENED the door of Bobby's, the local bar she and her friends liked to frequent, and paused for a moment, enjoying the crispness surrounding her.

It was one of those perfect end of summer evenings, warm during the day, but with the promise of fall in the air. She snuggled into her hoodie and smiled, thinking about how happy her brother, Sebastian, and his fiancée, Rachel, had been that evening at dinner.

Of course, a lot of that had to do with the fact that Rachel was sporting a diamond large enough to blind Kelsey . . . and the rest of the Earth's populace.

But, seriously, she was happy for them both.

Sebastian and Rachel were perfect for each other, and they deserved all the happiness in the world.

She slipped out of the opening and let the door start to close behind her, but before she got too far, Sebastian caught it. He slid through, dropped an arm around her shoulders. "Let me walk you to your car."

"I'm fine," she said, shrugging him off. "Go enjoy your fiancée. It's not your guys' fault that my flight is ridiculously early in the morning."

He rolled his eyes. "You know you're not going to win this argument, so just accept my chivalry. It's my brotherly duty, after all."

"You sell it so effectively."

"Shut up."

"*You* shut up."

"No, *you* shut up."

"*No—*"

They broke off with grins, and Kels let Bas sling his arm around her neck, tugging her into a hug. "I love you, brat," he told her.

"Well, *I* don't love you."

"Rude."

"You know it." But she hugged him back before leading him to her car. "I am really so happy for you both, you know that, right?"

"Of course, I do," he said.

They spent the next few minutes discussing the wedding—the date and location were set, as was the food—and the whole crew of females, including Kelsey, were going honeymoon shopping—because apparently that was a thing—the following week.

"It sounds like you've got it pretty much sorted."

Bas smiled. "Rachel's a force of nature," he joked. "Seriously, though, she wanted to ask you this, but I preferred to do it myself."

Kels frowned. "Ask me what?"

"To be a bridesmaid. We were hoping you'd be in the bridal party." He lifted his hands, palms up. "No pressure, of course, but we'd love to have you in the wedding."

No pressure? This was her brother. But her brother was a

reformed anti-social and so she understood the gesture—him asking her himself—for what it was. He wanted her there and it meant something. See? That M.S. in Neuroscience she had done in her spare time over the last few years had paid off—or at least the psychology classes that had been required for it had. She put her mental detour to the side and let her lips curve up. "I'm happy to play whatever role you want, Bas."

"How about flower girl?" he teased.

She shot him a glare. "Seriously?"

"So bridesmaid it is then?"

Since they'd reached her car, she unlocked the passenger's side door, and tossed her purse on the seat. "Yes," she murmured. "I'd be honored." Then added, a little firmer, so he'd know she was serious. "As long as you're sure that's what you guys want."

"I know this is all last minute," he said. "But it *is* what we want. We're ready to start our future together and want our family to be part of it."

Aw. Rachel was so good for him, bringing Bas out of his shell, making it so her brother could say something like that when he never would have managed it before.

"Thank you." She pressed a kiss to his cheek. "And count me in. Thank Rachel for me?" She'd call her future sis-in-law later to sort out dress details, but based on what she knew about Rach, Kels figured the dress was already purchased.

"Done."

Kels rounded her car, paused with her hand on the driver's door handle. "Oh, besides Devon"—their brother—"who are the other groomsmen?"

"We're keeping it small." He shrugged. "Heather is going to be the maid of honor, you a bridesmaid, and Devon is going to be my best man."

She smiled. "And Clay is going to be the other groomsman."

Bas shook his head.

Kelsey had opened her mouth, ready to tease Bas about choosing to include Rachel's boss over his when her gut sank.

Small bridal party.

Two on each side.

One of which was *not* Clay.

Her quiet, often taciturn brother only had a few close friends growing up. None of whom she could see in the bridal party.

Except one.

Fuck.

But she was worrying for nothing. Bas hadn't talked to Tanner in years as far as she knew. They *hadn't* talked in years. They couldn't have—

"Who is it then?" she asked through stiff lips.

Because it couldn't be Tanner. Her brother didn't know about them. She'd made sure of it. They'd kept things on the down-low and then when the short *thing* between them had gone bad . . . she'd nursed her broken heart two thousand miles away.

"Tanner."

Her gut twisted.

Double fuck.

And a shit for good measure.

"That's fine, right?" Bas asked. "You guys always seemed to get along great." Concern rippled across his face. "Is there something wrong? Did—?"

"No," she said quickly, fingers clenching on the roof of her car as she attempted to clear her expression of old pain while still keeping her tone light. "That's great. I'm sorry. I'm just preoccupied with my new project."

He grinned. "Always work with you."

"That's me," she said weakly. "Always working."

Of course, work was safer than risking another broken heart. Not that she wasn't fully over Tanner, because she was.

Definitely.

Liar, her big, juicy brain declared, never one to let anyone—including herself—hide from the truth.

Whatever.

"Great," Bas said. "Since you'll be paired up with him. And I know it's been a while, but he's coming into town next week to catch up." He tapped the roof of her car, took a step back. "You want to grab dinner with us?"

"I'd love to," she lied before getting into the car, and with a wave that hopefully didn't show her dismay, Kelsey drove away.

Paired up with Tanner.

Been there, done that.

Got the souvenir broken heart.

Triple fuck.

TWO

Tanner

HE SHOULDERED HIS CARRY-ON, smiled at the flight attendant who'd been flirting with him since the plane had crossed the Rockies, and strode off the plane. It had just been one in the latest of many flights, his job as a photojournalist having taken him all over the world.

But it was also the last of many in a way.

Because his career was over.

He was almost thirty, at the top of his field, and . . . he didn't want to do it anymore.

Bypassing the baggage claim carousel, Tanner exited the airport. Bas was waiting at the curb, huge grin on his face as he lowered the passenger's side window and gestured for him to get in.

"You look great, bro," he told his friend, and it was the truth. Bas was happier than Tanner had ever seen him.

"Rachel does a man good," Bas quipped.

"I can see that." Tanner shoved his bag into the backseat and buckled in. "How is the fiancée?"

"Working like a crazy person." But Bas grinned and his tone made it clear that Rachel's working habits didn't upset him. "She's allocated me exactly an hour tonight."

Tanner raised a brow.

Another flash of teeth. "She's clearing the decks for our honeymoon."

"Where are you guys going?"

"Aruba." Bas sighed. "The surf. White sand. And, more importantly, no cell phones."

"That bad?"

"Not bad," Bas said, navigating the airport's exit. "But Rach and I both have a hard time turning it off sometimes."

"I know the feeling," Tanner agreed. "Always seems to be one more thing to do, another project to squeeze in."

A punch to his arm. "Which is why I appreciate you coming to the wedding. I know your work schedule is just as crazy as ours. Where are you heading next? Antarctica? Some uninhabited part of the Amazon? Or, to keep with A's, Australia?"

Funny story, Tanner wasn't actually going anywhere.

That's what happened when a man burned out at the top of his career. Or at least, that was the route *he'd* taken, fucking idiot that he was.

He just hadn't told anyone yet.

"Well, actually—"

Bas's cell rang. "Oh, sorry, man. That's Rachel. I should make sure she's—"

"Don't have to explain to me," he said. "Pick up."

Since Bas had already pressed the button to answer the call, his reassurance was moot. Rachel's—or what he assumed was Rachel's—voice filled the car's speakers.

"Hey, babe," she said. "I grabbed a table. Has Tanner's flight landed yet?"

"Yup. His ass is currently plunked into the passenger's seat."

"Tell him to not mess with my settings," she said, laughter lacing her tone. "I just got the recline perfect."

"Hi," Tanner said. "That recline sounds serious. I'll be on my best behavior."

"Hi, Tanner," she said. "I'm kidding about the seat, obviously. Live vicariously and recline all you want."

"Noted," he said. "It's nice to meet you."

"You, too." She had a nice voice—warm and kind. "I'll let you two catch up, though I hope you like tacos."

"Love them," he replied, smirking inwardly because at heart he was a twelve-year-old boy. And also because after spending the last six months in the most remote parts of Southeast Asia, it had been way too long since he'd had tacos of any variety, food, female, or otherwise. "Carnitas?"

"Of course. This place has the best . . ."

They spent a few more minutes exchanging pleasantries before Rachel broke off. "*Oh!* Kels just walked in. I'm going to grab her. See you guys soon!"

Click.

But he barely registered the sound of Rachel hanging up.

Because—

"Kelsey's here, too?" he asked, gut twisting. He hadn't heard from her in years, random call almost a year back aside. She'd phoned out of the blue, apologizing for being a bitch to him in the past, for ruining things between them, when clearly *he'd* been the asshole who'd blown it and then hadn't been able to recognize that in time to get her back.

He'd assumed the call had come because she was drunk, though she'd assured him otherwise. But why she was holding on to guilt about their fling going south when she hadn't played any part didn't make any sense.

He should have known better.

He should have *done* better.

The only thing he could make sense of was that they were both young and impulsive, and while neither of them were so young anymore, Kelsey didn't appear to have grown out of the impulsiveness.

Bas smiled. "Yeah. It's great," he said. "She moved out here not too long ago, so I actually get to see her now and then." Another nudge of his shoulder against Tanner's. "You don't mind walking her down the aisle, do you?"

And considering Tanner had once contemplated that very same action—before he'd panicked and ruined things—he couldn't do anything but force a matching smile and nod.

"Of course, I don't mind."

Whether Kelsey would, was a completely different story.

THREE

Kelsey

TACOS.

The only reason she could get through that night.

Well, tacos and nacho cheese dip and prickly pear margaritas.

Fitting that her favorite alcoholic drink involved the word prickly, given that she was feeling exactly that way. Spiked. Barbed. Desperate to keep Tanner at a distance. Of course, that wasn't exactly necessary because he was doing an admirable job of keeping his own distance, but the intention was there, and she was sticking to it.

She didn't hate Tan anymore. Or . . . at least the mature part of her didn't.

However, the eighteen-year-old who'd loved him desperately enough to give up her lucrative job and follow him around the world still did.

But she was older now, an actual grown-up who understood that he'd prevented her from making a huge mistake.

Seeing him still stung though.

Especially when he had grown up in the nine years since she'd seen him. He'd filled out, muscled up, and had all sorts of interesting scruff and lines and scars on his face. And he was tan, a lovely olive color that her pale ass skin could never achieve, mostly because of genetics but also because of her life-style and being married to her computer and lab.

"Here you go," the waitress said softly, deftly snagging Kelsey's empty glass and replacing it with a full one, and totally proving that the hundred Kels had slipped her early on had been totally worth it.

"Thanks," she murmured.

"Absolutely." Then the pretty blonde was gone, and Kelsey was slurping down her fourth—fifth?—drink. A prickling on her nape had her glancing up.

Tanner.

Chocolate eyes locked on her. Disappointed, judgy choco-late eyes.

Because she was drinking?

Or because she was just a general disappointment?

And wow, *now* that was the alcohol talking. She normally was a one to two drink girl because alcohol went to her head. But prickly pear margaritas were the best, and so sometimes she went up to three.

Never four or five because then she got like this.

Self-hating.

But if she managed to get to six, she was the freaking life of the party.

To hurry the process along, she chugged like she was in college again . . . or, well, she chugged pretending she'd been of legal—or near legal—age while she'd been in college.

A glass of water appeared in front of her.

"Drink."

Her eyes flicked up and, full disclosure, she lost herself in those judgy chocolate eyes for a good thirty seconds.

Tequila.

But then her favorite server in the history of all servers appeared next to her, and just like the genie from *Aladdin*, managed to swap out the empty for another full glass before Kelsey blinked.

Tanner, however, wasn't as impressed by her skills. He snagged her arm, ordering, "No more."

Yeah, no. He didn't get to do that. Ever.

"How many have I had?" she asked the waitress.

She opened her mouth, but he beat her to answer. "Six."

Kel glanced at the waitress, who nodded in agreement.

Damn.

She'd been hoping it had been five.

Six drinks was her limit, but not because Tanner had declared it. Six was her limit because seven meant she'd go from the life of the party to the puker of the party, and *that* was not a role she wanted to play.

"I'm done," she told the waitress, "but not because this asshole ordered it. I'm done because I don't want to upchuck at my brother's celebration."

The waitress nodded, lips twitching. "Seems like a good call."

Kels reached into her pocket and pulled out another hundred. "Thanks for being awesome. Water from here on out."

"You don't have—" The waitress tried to hand the money back, but Kelsey took her fingers and closed them around the bill.

"Next night off, enjoy a few drinks of your choice on me."

A beat of hesitation before she nodded and shoved the bill in her apron pocket. Then she made her away around the table, checking glasses and bringing more chips before announcing the entrees would be out any minute.

And all the while Tan stood by Kelsey's chair.

Since she'd chugged the previous, she made sure to savor this one. So freaking delicious—tart but sweet and cold enough that it slid down her throat with nary a burn.

Hence the reason she could suck them back like glasses of water, but also the reason they seemed to sneak up on her, if her spinning head was any indication. She grabbed a handful of chips, ignoring Tanner's glowering presence at her shoulder.

"Trying to kill yourself?" he muttered.

She glanced up at him sweetly. "Hi, Tanner. Lovely to see you. Hope your worldly travels have been fantastic." A beat. "Now, kindly *travel* your ass over to the other side of the table and leave me alone."

Fire in his eyes.

And not the good kind.

The lashing out, stinging type she'd felt that night nine years ago. The kind of verbal laceration that someone *never* forgot.

Or at least, she hadn't.

Her stomach clenched, preparing herself for the hit.

"Glad to see you haven't changed."

She'd had practice with this, dealing with asshole men of all sizes and shapes, so she knew she revealed nothing. Kelsey had grown up in a lot of ways over the years, but the biggest of which was getting really good at hiding her pain.

Tanner had taught her that.

How to pretend everything was perfect and amazing, even while her world was collapsing around her.

"Thank you," she said. "I hate to think I had gray hairs and wrinkles already."

Lame.

Not that she had any gray hairs, or visible ones anyway, because her stylist had her back and dyed those little fuckers immediately upon appearance.

He opened his mouth, but she managed to fake a little better. "I have, however, grown out of obsessing over the Jonas Brothers, even if I do love their new music. Prince Harry"—she put her hands over her heart—"he'll always be part of me here."

Bas nudged her shoulder, and she could have kissed him for his perfect timing. "Stop waxing poetic about your princely love and pass me the chips."

She scooped up a handful and plunked them on her plate before doing her sisterly duty and relinquishing the chips. "You know how much I love you, right?" she said, sufficiently drunk enough to move on from self-hate and diving right into the life-of-the-party stage. Which basically meant she teased and then enjoyed being teased back. Luckily, the parties involved— perhaps with the lone exception of Tanner—thought she was hilarious in this state. Apparently, it was the only time she let loose enough to not get her tender feelings hurt over said teasing.

Which may or may not be true.

Fine, it probably *was* true because she did like to dish it out, but often had a hard time taking it. Not fair, she knew, but Kels was well aware she wasn't perfect.

"Just saying, only the best sister in your family would be nice enough to offer you their chips."

"You're my only sister."

"Details, details."

Bas smirked. "Also, pretty sure they're the table's chips."

She shook her head. "Personal baskets."

"What?"

"There are ten baskets and ten of us," she said. "Hence, personal baskets." Oh, look. Her drink was right there. She might as well finish it. But when she went to lift it to her lips, Tanner was there, arms crossed and glaring down at her.

"There are not—"

Bas broke off, probably counting.

Meanwhile, she turned to Tanner and matched his glare, though his higher position meant she had to glare up, while he got to glare down, and everyone knew that glaring down was the better strategic position.

Tan opened his mouth, and Kelsey realized she really was drunker than she'd realized. Her normal mental tangents and taken her down a few very strange rabbit holes in the last minutes.

Personal baskets of chips.

Yikes. Time for some water.

She set the margarita down, feeling sad for wasting the deliciousness of the prickly pear, and picked up the glass of water.

"You know that cocktail doesn't have actual feelings, right?"

"Why are you still here?" she snapped.

Uh-oh.

Tanner's expression went deadly, but she'd drunk enough that her normally meager filters were gone. Finished. Done-zo.

"Excuse me?"

"You heard me," she said. "You didn't want me then, so you don't get to talk to me now."

The table had been loud and raucous up until the moment she said that, or rather *yelled* it. But all night, the restaurant had been beyond noisy, music blaring, people chatting and laughing, plates and silverware clanking. Yet, the moment those words crossed her lips, silence reigned. The music was between songs, conversations had lulled, and everyone heard that Tanner hadn't wanted her.

Everyone.

Including Bas.

Her brother's face clouded. *"What did you say?"*

She stifled a curse, the buzz of alcohol creeping away from the edges of her mind and letting soberness claw its way in. If she'd thought Tanner's glare had been deadly before, now it was positively nuclear.

Fuck.

Her laugh was forced and loud. "I'm kidding," she said, shoving Tanner's arm. It made her head spin, and that was *only* the alcohol talking, definitely not the fact that the contact had sent tingles up her arm. "Oh, look!" she announced at large. "Food's here! Thank goodness. Those margaritas are deadly."

More laughter, awkward on her part, gentle on the part of her soon-to-be sister-in-law's friends.

The Sextant, as they'd dubbed themselves—and they were fully aware that wasn't the proper term for a group of six, but apparently too much wine at book club had led to them googling while intoxicated and misnaming themselves. Still, it had stuck, and Kels had even gone to a few of their so-called book clubs. They were fun, beautiful women both inside and out.

But she also knew that she'd just prickled their drama-seeking antennae with that loud declaration.

Hell would be paid.

Though, not as much as what Tanner would be enduring from her brother, if Bas's expression was any indication.

However, the friendly server once again saved the day, moving around the table with practiced speed and depositing plates at regular intervals, including stepping between her and Tanner to set her food down. He shifted back to let the blonde beauty in—Kels really needed to find out her name because she owed a serious debt of womanhood—then he glared down at her for one more long moment before turning on heel and going down to his end of the table.

If only that end could be a little further away.

Say, Antarctica.

Yeah, he'd fit in with the penguins down there.

Kels smirked, imagining him waddling around and sitting on an egg for months at a time. He was patient, was well used to being still while waiting for that perfect shot. Further that, he'd *always* been patient. Not just behind the lens, but in bed, then at outwaiting her until she gave up on them as a them.

She'd picked up her taco while thinking those lovely thoughts, chowing down on the carne asada and whitefish varieties she craved on a regular basis because they were just that good, when the memory of how he'd out-patienced her reared its ugly head.

Suddenly the tacos weren't so tasty.

Cardboard had more on them. And maybe some shards of broken glass.

Or perhaps nuclear waste.

Whatever it was, the memory of Tanner breaking up with her, of his cruel words and her response to them—strike back, strike *hard*—brought the two emotions that always seemed to be roiling beneath the surface straight to the top of the pile.

Embarrassment and shame.

Cute.

Sighing, she set down the taco and pushed up from her chair.

"Be right back," she murmured to Bas when he looked up.

His brows drew down. "You okay?"

A forced smile, that really good one she'd perfected. "Yup." Her shrug was self-deprecating. "Too many liquids."

He relaxed and turned his attention back to Rachel, who was sitting on his other side, not taking long for his focus to be only her. As it should be. This was their night. But his concern for Kels, checking in, watching out for her—she was lucky enough that it was like that with all the male members of her family. Dev, Bas, and her dad were just really good people, always looking out for the people around them, loving the ones who had a piece of their heart without reservation. Even when Bas had gone through his distant stage, he'd still been kind and considerate and protective.

And she'd never resented the care.

Mostly because being in the spotlight of it didn't feel like she was stuck in a jail cell, but also because she and her mom gave that same care back. Having been in one relationship that had been on the wrong side of that line, when protection had felt smothering, was a life experience that made sure she knew and appreciated the difference fully now.

Lucky for her, she'd gotten smart and dumped the guy.

Even though the bathroom wasn't actually her stop, Kelsey didn't risk drawing attention by going for her jacket as she walked from the table. Instead, she left it and slipped down the hall that lead to the back doors of the restaurant.

There was a tiny patio there, and while it was often packed on summer days and evenings, this fall night was too cold. The chairs were stacked along one wall, the umbrellas collapsed, and the tables were topped with condensation. But it was quiet, and for her rapidly sobering brain—*thanks to you for that, memories* —it gave her a moment to breathe.

Clear enough to see the stars and cold enough that her breath fogged in front of her, Kelsey leaned back against the wall and closed her eyes.

Breathe. Just breathe.

It was going to be fine. Everything would work out the way it was supposed to, and just because she was the single Scott who couldn't seem to find a person to love her for all her flaws, didn't mean she was going to die alone in her apartment with her seventy-two cats eating her face off.

Nope.

It'd probably be her seventy-two dogs, because she was much more of a dog person.

Speaking of that, maybe she'd get a dog. A cute little corgi with stumpy legs and a stretched-out body. Then again, dogs were a lot of work and she could hardly complete her own. Then again, *again*, Heather O'Keith had been bugging her to hire a few more lab assistants and punt off some of her grunt work.

Then again, again, *again,* she was purposely distracting herself from the real thing bothering her.

Tanner and the fact that she still had it bad for him.

His gorgeous face, the hint of a dimple on his left cheek, the bump on the top of his nose from a basketball injury in high school—and yes, she'd been at the game because she'd gone to *all* his games—the way his hair always looked a little disheveled, as though he'd just run his hands through it. How he smiled gently when people spoke to him, no matter if it was a stranger on the street asking for the time or Bas telling him a funny work story.

How he'd hugged.

How he'd kissed her.

How he'd taken her virginity—

"You aren't going to puke, are you?"

FOUR

Tanner

FUCK, she *was* going to throw up.

Her face was pale, no hint of the lovely peaches and cream coloration he'd spent way too many nights dreaming about after they'd—*he'd*—broken things off. Her lids peeled back, and her brown eyes were slightly hazy.

Brown wasn't the right description of those eyes, the one word could not nearly begin to encompass the breadth of color and depth. More whiskey than mocha, but with hints of espresso running through, and the right one had a perfect gray ring around its pupil. Hell, he figured he knew Kelsey's eyes better than his own. He'd sketched them, photographed them, stared into them while naked and felt way too many emotions for a boy who'd had nothing and suddenly felt everything.

Her eyes closed again. "I'm fine," she said, and the tone was *almost* perfect. If he hadn't known her so well in a past life, it might have fooled him. Especially when she added, "Just trying to puzzle out a work problem." A beat, lips curving but lids staying shut. "As one does."

He leaned against the wall next to her, seeing her stiffen, but Tanner had to give it to her, she didn't move away, didn't do anything but stay where she was and keep breathing.

"What's the problem?" he asked after a few minutes.

"What?"

"The work problem you're puzzling."

Her lips tipped up into a faint smile. "Oh, I puzzled that already. We were missing a critical line of code." She shrugged, as if her solving a work problem was as easy as breathing. And knowing her and how brilliantly smart she was, it probably was just that easy.

"So, now, what's your excuse for being out here?"

Silence, pretty eyes on his. "Because I can never seem to tear myself away from you." Her mouth curved into a rueful smile. "Though *you* don't seem to have that problem."

He jerked, opened his mouth to say something, but nothing came. The words stoppered up in his throat, and he could only stare at her like an imbecile.

"Though," she said. "I think you actually did me a favor. Made me grow up. Helped me learn when to suck it up and cut my losses." She pushed off the wall. "Everyone has a first heartbreak, the one that teaches you how things can go bad. I think I was lucky that I had you doing the breaking. Someone else, and I might have ended up doing something really stupid." Her fingers found his forearm and squeezed. "Thanks for looking out for me."

And then she was gone, the spots she'd touched burning, but the hole in his heart an absolute crater.

―――――

By the time he made it back inside, Tanner was a little more centered. Kelsey was, too. Or at the very least, she was beautiful and laughing and putting on a great show for all parties involved.

"Then," she said, the story not breaking its pace as he took his seat, "Bas came out of the bathroom, teeny tiny washcloth over his manly bits, the only white part left on his body."

Rachel and her posse cackled.

"And he was *all* green?" the pretty brunette he thought was named Abby asked.

"Yes!" Kels laughed. "Devon and I replaced his body wash and shampoo with animal-safe dye. He looked like a stalk of broccoli, skinny but with his mop of hair flopping all over the place."

Bas grinned good-naturedly. "I don't know what I was thinking, bleaching my hair that summer."

"Me neither." Kels smiled back at her brother. "But those blond locks really made the green dye pop."

"Brat." But he tossed his arm over her shoulders and reached up a fist to noogie her hair. "Only took me about thirty showers to get it so I could leave the house and not look like an alien."

Kels squirmed away. "Green is not your color."

Bas shook his head. "You and Devon put me through the wringer, you know that, right?"

Rachel rolled her eyes. "No playing the martyr, love. I seem to remember a certain brother who took all of his sister's stuffed animals and held them for ransom. Not to mention replacing the tip of your lovely sister's eyeliner with that of a permanent marker."

"That was in response to the broccoli incident!"

Tanner snorted.

First, because he'd bleached his hair that summer, too, and second, because he'd seen the outcome of both pranks.

The Scotts were vicious.

Case in point, when Bas pointed across the table and declared, "And Tanner, I thought he was my friend, but it turned out he was in on all of them."

"What?" Kelsey's eyes flicked to his.

"He gave Devon the dye *and* he thought of the eyeliner prank."

Ice from her end of the table. "And what about Mr. Snuggles? He never recovered from his incarceration."

Meaning, he and Bas had accidentally shoved Mr. Snuggles in an access panel for some plumbing, not realizing that the pipes got really hot and that the synthetic fur of Kelsey's favorite unicorn toy would melt.

She'd cried when they'd returned the misshapen toy, and he'd never felt more like an ass.

Except perhaps when he'd broken things off with her.

"I was in on that, too."

Definite frost, but she continued putting on her show, and so her lips curved. "You monster."

"No brothers and sisters to torment meant I had to find my own way."

Some of that ice melted, her knowing what it had been like growing up in his house. Not an uncommon story, his upbringing. Parents who worked too much, who spent all their time either uninvolved in his life, or feeling guilty for not being there and suffocating him.

At first, he'd eaten up the attention, been so starved for it.

But then work would inevitably become more important, and he'd been shuttled to after-school care or, once he'd become friends with Bas, the Scotts had let him hang out at their house every afternoon.

Sebastian's mom was the best, framing it like he was doing them a favor so Bas wouldn't be alone while she shuttled Dev to hockey practice and Kelsey to her extra academic courses. He hadn't cared why they'd let him stay. Besides Bas being his best friend, meaning extra hang out time was great, he'd also just loved being part of the hustle and bustle of a big family. Cars coming and going, voices talking over each other at the dinner table, laughter and teasing echoing through the halls.

His house was quiet.

Bigger and undoubtedly fancier than the Scotts', but so much colder.

No soul.

The only good thing his parents had ever done for him, besides the whole feeding and clothing and giving him a safe place to live—because those couldn't be discounted, even if he had been neglected in almost every other way—was buy him a camera. But after spending fourteen years shooting profession-ally, nine of those moving from place to place, never settling down, never having a home base for more than a couple of weeks, now he wondered how much he'd missed out on while using his job, his cameras as a shield.

Intimacy for sure.

At first, there had been lots of women, but that had gotten old quick.

At first, he'd loved flitting from place to place without being tied down.

But eventually he'd begun to miss home, to miss the noisy Scotts, to miss Kelsey and her brain that never stopped.

That had been a year before.

That had been because Kelsey had called.

He'd been looking through the lens of his camera, searching for the perfect shot, the perfect composition that would fill the hole inside him, and her phone call had made him see.

It would never be filled.

Not with photography, anyway.

He wanted to come home. He wanted to see his friends, his family—that would be the Scotts, not his biological parents.

And . . . he needed to see her.

To find out if it was the same.

The gnawing need, the draw that seemed to never waver, even though he'd done his best to stretch it to snapping by moving all around the world. Because he'd known at twenty-one, and he knew now.

Kelsey was it for him.

And just like then, that knowledge was absolutely terrifying.

Laughter drew him out of his head, the conversation having carried on while he'd been deep in thought. He reached for his beer and slugged back a fair portion of it.

"Got it bad," came a voice from his right. It was New York through and through and belonged to a gray-eyed beauty whose blond hair and gorgeous looks no doubt made most men underestimate her.

Tan didn't, however.

He saw the sharpness in her gaze, the shrewdness in her expression. That, paired with the fact that she was one of the most famous lawyers in the country at the moment—having won a big case against a corporation who was taking advantage of their hourly employees, a case that was currently all over television—meant that he knew Bec Darden to be a very smart human.

"Heard about your case," he said. "That was huge."

A flash of white teeth. "Thanks," she said. "But your pathetic attempts at distraction don't work with me."

"Becky baby," her husband, Luke, said. "This isn't the courtroom. Let the man enjoy his beer."

The fierce lawyer wrinkled her nose. "But he's got it bad."

"Anyone within a three-mile radius can see that, but still, the man should get to enjoy his beer."

Tanner sighed.

"But—"

"And I think I've had enough of tonight," Tanner muttered and stood, crossing to his friend and Rachel. "Sorry to say, but jet lag is hitting hard."

Bas started to stand. "I can drop you at your hotel."

Tanner shook his head. "Stay. I'll just grab my bag from your car and call a Lyft."

Sebastian's eyes flicked toward Kelsey, who was laughing with Abby. "Actually, maybe you can drive Kels home? She mentioned her car is here, and she doesn't want to drink and drive. If you take her, she wouldn't have to come and grab it in the morning. Her apartment is just a couple of blocks from your hotel."

Sensible.

But hellish.

And yet, what could he say aside from, "Sure. Sounds like a plan."

"If you even still have a valid license."

Tan rolled his eyes. "I do."

"And you've driven something more than a horse and wagon over the last year."

"Does a Range Rover count?"

It was Sebastian's turn to roll his eyes. "Always so fancy."

"All I got."

A snort before Bas turned to his sis and said, "Tanner will drive you home so you don't have to come back for your car tomorrow."

"I'm just going to get a—"

"You just told me you were leaving. Tanner is jet-lagged and needs to get to his hotel." Bas smiled. "Two birds, one stone."

Tan watched as Kelsey considered her options.

It didn't take her as long as him to realize they didn't have any. Either she went with this and pretended it was no big deal for a family friend to drive her home, or she admitted she didn't want to be trapped in a car with Tanner and why that was.

She chose option one.

Plastering on her fake smile, she pushed back her chair and stood. On went the jacket, waves and goodbyes were extended all around, a hug to Abby, to her brother, to Rachel, then she scooped up her purse and turned for the front of the restaurant.

Tanner followed her, but not before he saw the knowing expression on Bec and Luke's faces.

Yup.

He had it bad.

And he had the feeling that pretty soon everyone was going to know that.

FIVE

Kelsey

HELL.

A full seven circles.

Or maybe eight.

Ten?

Maybe *that* was a little far, after all. She may be trapped in a car with Tan, but it wasn't like he was driving them over a cliff. In fact, he seemed to be maneuvering very carefully through the streets of the city.

They hadn't talked except for her to give him the address.

Which was perhaps that eighth circle.

Sexual tension—on her part. Memories. Heartbreak.

Maybe ten wasn't so out there after all.

But traffic wasn't terrible, and they were nearing her place. Soon she could change into the cozy pajamas that Rachel had gotten her hooked on, down some water and preventative ibuprofen so she didn't die tomorrow when she had to get up for work, and then turn on *Outlander*.

She was way behind and needed to get caught up before she got together with her friends on Friday.

Spoilers were the worst.

Right behind the silence in this car.

They slid to a stop at a red light, her staring out the window, him with his eyes on the road.

"Did I ever apologize to you?" he said.

Shit. Why hadn't she turned on the radio? At least if she had, she could have pretended not to hear him. Instead, all she had was silence and a rapidly rising pulse.

Turn green. Turn green. Turn—

Fingers on her cheek.

"Kels."

She kept her eyes pointed out the window, the prickly pear goodness was totally gone now, but she answered him. "No."

A curse. "I'm an asshole."

No denying that.

He chuckled darkly. "I'm guessing you agree."

"Light's green."

The car moved. "Definitely agree."

Kels sighed and leaned back against the seat. "Fuck, Tan, what do you expect? We spent the summer fooling around and hiding things from my parents and my brothers while you promised me we were building something more, something permanent." She shook her head, hair catching on the fabric of her seat. "I know we were young and both made mistakes and that I reacted to you leaving like a spoiled brat. But I've apologized for that, and it also doesn't change the fact that"—another sigh, her voice dropping—"you said we were more—"

He'd said she was *everything.*

"—and then you just threw it away." Threw *her* away.

"You're right."

She froze, having expected him to latch onto the young and made mistakes part rather than agreeing with her.

"Yes, I was young and too fucking stupid to recognize exactly how good I had it. And"—he glanced in the mirror, changed lanes—"I was also a scared asshole who panicked because I had it so good. My head was messed up, Kels. My teenage and college fantasies were about you, and yet I spent every day pretending to just be your brother."

Yeah, that *had* been a little strange.

She'd never thought of Tanner as her brother, but they had pretended their relationship was like that when her family was there. Partly because it was fun to sneak around, but mostly because they were too young and cowardly to declare themselves a couple.

Her brothers wouldn't have liked it, and she didn't think her parents would have either, considering exactly how much time Tan and she had spent alone.

"We made a mess," she said softly.

He snorted. "Yeah. A big one."

"I liked the time we spent together."

And just when she thought the prickly pear was out of her, she had to go and admit that. Kels bit her tongue until it stung, reading Tanner's silence for exactly what it was. He'd liked it, too, but there was no going back.

"Like I said," she added as he pulled into her underground garage, "it sucks that it went down that way, but it also was probably for the best."

More silence. This time she didn't break it with her blathering.

"My spot's on the left. Six down."

He parked, and she stifled a sigh. "Thanks for driving me back. If you're going to walk, I'll let you into the lobby so you can cut through to your hotel." Her gaze drifted up and over to his.

He nodded.

Great.

She popped the door and hopped out, reaching back in and between the seats in order to grab her coat and work bag. The first went over her arm, the second . . . got snagged from her hand.

"I've got it," Tanner said, gripping the rather large tote like it was a clutch. She shivered. It might have been nine years, but she distinctly remembered the feel of his touch, the sensation of those big, calloused fingers trailing down her skin, slipping between her thighs—

La. La. La.

Kels needed to focus and not on how good Tanner had been in bed, or how off the charts their chemistry had been.

She'd had good sex over the years. Not great. But it had been pretty damned good. Plus, she had *Outlander* to look forward to and a set of really good vibrators that would make her Jamie experience even better.

Tan reached across her and closed the door. Then he clicked the locks, handed her the keys, tossed his own bag over his shoulder, and picked up his duffle.

Her signal to move so they could get this over with.

And since she had her Jamie and her Platinum—yes, her vibrator was named after the precious metal and no joke, it was worth as much as a bar of the stuff—to look forward to, she sucked in a breath and led the way over to the elevators. Security in her building was good. She had to swipe her card to access the room with the elevators and then swipe it again to get the elevator to move.

She hit the buttons for the lobby and her floor, and a few seconds later, the doors opened to reveal the marble-floored space. Kels put her hand out to prevent it from closing back up then pointed. "Just go out the doors and to the left. Your hotel is two blocks down." Tanner glanced in that direction and nodded, but didn't get off.

She raised a brow.

"I'll walk you up first."

"I don't need—"

His expression went mulish, and she knew it was either spend the next five minutes fighting with him and knowing that any argument she might put up would be ignored anyway, or she could just accept that he was going to walk her up and then get on with her evening.

Rolling her eyes, she let go and stepped back, allowing the elevator doors to close and the metal death box to rise the six floors to her apartment.

"You didn't use to give in so easily."

She leaned back against the wall and stifled a sigh, since they would counteract her next words. "Meet new and improved me."

Half of Tanner's mouth tipped up, but his gaze drifted down to her toes, and if she wasn't totally mistaken, Kels would say there was heat in those chocolate depths. But then again, she was probably just delusional due to the prickly pear's yummi-ness. "Improved how?"

She glanced down then thought—thanks prickly pear—what the fuck? Her hands came up and she cupped her breasts, jabbing herself in the left one with her keys. *Ow.* "These are new since I've seen you."

Tanner choked. "You got implants?"

A frown dragged her brows down. "No," she said. "Pig."

The doors dinged open, and he held them for her. "Just saying, I'm not the one cupping them and drawing attention to the hottest set of tits I've seen in ages."

She couldn't fault him for that.

Dropping her hands, she moved off the elevator. "My point was," she said, "that I've grown up since I last saw you."

He moved so he was walking next to her. "Grown up or filled out?"

This made her snort, and she punched him before admitting, "Both."

"Yeah," he said softly, "I noticed. What else has changed in nine years?"

"Hmm," she said, slowing her pace. Her head wasn't fuzzy, and she had gotten over her embarrassment with Tan. All that was left of her night was a pleasant warm sensation in her stomach from the cocktails. Or maybe that was just Tanner. "I've got my own place," she told him. Her apartment was around the corner, the last one in the hall. Although it was smaller than the other units on the floor, the placement in the building meant that she had lovely views of the bay.

"That is very grown-up," he said. "I don't have an apartment." At her look, he added, "Got rid of mine after a while. Was paying for a place that I was never in and so when I come home, I usually just bunk on someone's couch."

"Bas never mentioned you staying with him."

"Probably because I've been home to the states maybe six times since I left, and four of those were for jobs." There was a hint of something in his tone that she couldn't place in his expression, but then his face cleared, and he nodded at the door they'd stopped in front of. "This you?"

She nodded. "Yup."

Her keys were slipped from her fingers and before she knew it, the door was open, and he was nudging her inside. Immediately, because it was the first thing she always did when walking into her apartment, Kels stepped out of her heels and pushed them to the side. In proximity to the shoe rack her neat freak of a friend, Heidi, had bought her, but not on it.

His eyes slipped to her feet, and she glanced down to see her bright pink nails.

There those lips went again, curving upward just the slightest bit, even as his gaze seemed to be cataloging everything about her. Damn. Why did he have to be even sexier than before? Broader shoulders, slender hips, fine lines on the outside of his eyes that spoke to him having spent at least part of the last nine years laughing. His skin was tan and when he lounged back against the doorway crossing his arms, she noticed a tattoo on the inside of his forearm.

"What else has changed, Kels?"

She turned and walked further into her apartment, hanging up her coat, pulling out her laptop and plugging it into the charger she had on her kitchen counter. Then she stepped to her sink, reached into the cabinet, and pulled out a glass.

She held it up in his direction. "I have matching glassware? Want some lemonade?"

His half-smile went full, and he stepped into the apartment, closing the door behind him. "So, some things haven't changed, have they? Do you still make your lemonade with approximately two pounds of sugar?" He prowled toward her, and Kels's heart skipped a beat.

"Maybe just a pound now." She shrugged and grabbed another cup, setting it on the counter before turning toward the fridge to retrieve her pitcher of lemonade. "I haven't seemed to be able to grow out of my sweet tooth."

"Hmm."

Two glasses poured, she returned the pitcher and handed him one. "Thanks for the ride." A beat. "In my car. With my gas. But thanks anyway, I suppose."

"Just remember me when you don't have to get up early in the morning to go and get it." He took a sip and winced.

"Still too sweet?"

"There are some things that can never be too sweet," he murmured, reaching past her to place the cup on the counter, and she knew he wasn't talking about food or drink so much as people. Or maybe her?

But he'd left.

"How's work?" she murmured, pushing that thought away.

The change that overtook him was instant and all-encompassing.

Relaxed shoulders stiffened, softened jaw clenched, lips pressed flat, and his eyes . . . those went cold, frostier than a chocolate shake. "Fine."

Since that *fine* both spoke to things not being at all fine and also him putting up several rolls of caution tape, Kelsey set down her own glass and brushed by him, heading toward the door.

"For what it's worth," she said. "I'm glad you drove me home and we got to talk. Will make that trip down the aisle a lot easier."

He'd been lost in thought for a moment but jolted as her words reached him.

Then his head came up, and he closed the distance between them. "Thanks for the drink."

A nod.

"Apartment's nice."

Another nod, and he reached for the door.

"Tanner?"

"Yes, baby?" He was distracted by whatever was in his brain and probably didn't mean that baby at all, but the endearment was enough for her filter-less, impulsive tongue.

"About the car—" He frowned, so she hurried to add,

"About remembering you doing me a favor by driving me home—"

"Baby, I was just kidding about that."

Another baby. *Really* distracted. Still, she kept going.

"I didn't need the reminder to think of you," she admitted. "I've thought of you every single day since you left me."

It was as though he'd suddenly been prodded with electricity. Every muscle in his body went taut, and he rotated to face her. "What did you say?"

Oh shit.

She shook her head. "Forget it—"

He kissed her.

One second, she was ready to run away or beg the floor to swallow her up so she could forget what she'd admitted, and the next moment his mouth was on hers, his tongue down her throat, and sparks exploding along her spine.

Her knees wobbled, her panties got soaked, and her arms slid around his neck.

Hell, she was never going to catch up on *Outlander* now.

SIX

Tanner

FUCK, had it always been this good between them?

Tan had thought it was pretty freaking great kissing Kels nine years before, but now his mouth on hers was fucking incendiary. He slid his tongue across the seam of her mouth, and she opened immediately, letting him in at the same time she wrapped her arms around his neck and tugged him closer.

She tasted of tequila and flowers, sweet with tang, but she also tasted of Kelsey.

His Kelsey.

His from the first time he'd laid eyes on her, eight years old with tears in those pretty brown eyes because she'd fallen and scraped her knee. He hadn't known what she was to him then, just that he hadn't liked seeing her hurt and crying, so he'd hugged her and helped her inside to her mom.

But she'd been his since that moment.

That hadn't changed when he was in middle school and she was taking college courses, books sprawled on her kitchen island and pencil marks on her face. He hadn't been able to help her with her homework—in fact, she usually helped *him* when his own math problems stumped him—but he'd been self-sufficient for a long time. He knew how to make good snacks, and since she'd often forget to eat when completing whatever complicated work her professors had assigned her, Tan had made it his responsibility to feed her.

Even when they'd gotten older, when he and Bas had spent more time out of the Scott house than in it, he'd still checked in on her.

She'd been pretty then, but still so young, and he'd been in high school then college and after what most boys that age were. Kels had been both jailbait and his best friend's sister, so she was beyond off-limits. She was absolutely, impenetrably untouchable.

He'd tucked away the *pretty*, focused on the *sister* . . . until the day she'd graduated with her Master's, and he'd made the mistake of hugging her.

So right in his arms. So much fiery desire from such innocent contact.

Like now—

But also unlike now.

Because his mouth was on hers, and she was kissing him with far more confidence than she'd ever done before.

Her fingers drifted to his head and wove into the strands of his hair, tugging firmly, making prickles of pain dance on his scalp. Rather than really hurting, it enhanced, taking his cock from mostly hard to granite and sending his control scattering.

His hands swept down and cupped her ass, scooping her up. She didn't hesitate to wrap her legs around his waist and, fuck, that felt incredible. Lungs screaming for oxygen, he broke from her mouth, sucking in air while nipping at her throat, running his tongue along the shell of her ear. She moaned when he sucked on the lobe, fingers clenching on his scalp again, and he felt a bolt of satisfaction in remembering her spots, in discovering they hadn't changed.

But he also knew this was too much too soon, so he didn't drift lower when he desperately wanted to. Instead, he went back to her mouth, nibbling at the corner before taking it in a slow, easy kiss that helped him garner some of the tendrils of his control. Finally, he eased back, returning to reality to find that he'd pinned her against the wall, his groin nestled against the sweet softness of her pussy, and that reality meant that his control almost went scattering again.

Luckily—or perhaps *un*luckily, depending on how one looked at it—Tan glanced to the right and saw the eight-by-ten of her family hanging on the wall less than a foot from her head.

The whole gang was there, her parents, Grant and Megan, Devon and his wife, Becca, Sebastian and Rachel, and Kelsey. Brown locks shining, huge smile on her beautiful face, and bright brown eyes proudly focused on the camera.

Everyone else was laughing, no doubt because she'd said something smart ass.

They were happy.

And he wasn't there.

Carefully, Tanner set Kelsey back on her feet, trying to ignore the piercing pain that reminded him of exactly how much he'd missed when he'd run. It took her a moment to come to, her lids opening slowly to reveal eyes hazed with desire. His cock twitched again, but he ignored it and stepped back after making sure she was steady.

That made the haze clear slightly and a pang of regret shot through him, but seriously, what the fuck had he been thinking? He was fucked up. He didn't have a job, had put his camera equipment in storage—or all but his favorite DSLR—and he didn't even have a place to stay. Spending the last years as a nomad meant that he didn't have any ties, didn't know how to be part of a family, let alone a close one like the Scotts, and he knew that the moment he got involved with Kelsey, he'd be all in.

Which meant that inevitably he'd fuck things up with her.

And then he'd lose what he had with *all* the Scotts.

"Fuck," he muttered, turning away and shoving a hand through his hair. He needed them in his life, needed *Kelsey* in his life, and that meant he had to get a handle on this desire and go back to being a surrogate brother. If he didn't, he'd lose them all.

"Good to know that my kissing still makes you react in the same way."

At that smart comment, he almost turned around and slammed his mouth back down on hers. It took locking every muscle in his body tight to keep from doing it, but he managed. Then he sucked in a breath, took two steps, and reached for the doorknob.

He heard a noise—a rustle, a whoosh of something falling to the floor.

He shouldn't have looked. He knew that in his bones.

But he also knew he couldn't have *not* looked to save his life.

Tanner had made the same mistake all those years ago—underestimating Kels—and why he did the same thing in that moment was beyond fucking stupid. Regardless of his mental capacity, he glanced back.

Oh fuck.

She was standing opposite him . . . wearing nothing but her bra and panties.

He looked. He had to *fucking* look.

Turquoise lace that did nothing to disguise the dusky pink of her nipples, the brown hair between her thighs. Her breasts and hips were larger. She'd been slender before, almost a reed of a girl, but now she was all woman. Still tall and thin, but with curves that his palms ached to caress.

"Tan," she murmured.

He was frozen.

Then she unhooked her bra and dropped it to the floor.

Fuck.

Her breasts, holy shit, he'd thought the lace hadn't concealed much, but he'd been wrong. Seeing them naked, bouncing softly as she moved toward him, was going to be burned into his brain for all eternity.

She closed the distance between them, getting close enough that her breasts brushed his chest. Hard nipples through the cotton of his T-shirt, floral scent of her hair, soft breath catching in the back of his throat. His hands were in fists at his sides, desperate to touch her and yet terrified of what might happen if he did.

A kiss to his throat, floral scent getting closer, inundating his senses when she rose on tiptoe and whispered in his ear, "Come to bed."

Then she dropped back down and turned, fingers slipping into the waistband of her underwear, hips doing a little shimmy that did absolutely fantastic things to her ass, and that turquoise lace hit the floor.

Hot brown eyes over her shoulder, shining brown locks dancing on her back.

He took a step forward and he watched her smile grow.

Then she disappeared through a doorway that no doubt led to her bedroom.

Tanner took another step.

But his gaze caught on the family portrait again, and he froze. He had to leave, and he had to leave in that moment. Otherwise he was going to cave, walk into that bedroom, then make love to Kelsey in every single way he'd imagined over the last nine years.

Which meant they'd probably never leave.

But it also meant that he would have ruined things.

He spun, scrambled for the doorknob, opted for the stairs, and hustled his way out onto the street. It wasn't running. Rather, it was him protecting the most precious thing in the universe.

Or at least, that's what he told himself to convince him to keep walking.

SEVEN

Kelsey

SHE SIPPED her one beer slowly, because after her experience with six prickly pear margaritas, she'd decided to take it easy on alcohol.

As in, she was never drinking tequila again.

Beer made her a little loopy after one or two glasses, but tequila made her stupid.

Or maybe that was just because she'd had six.

Either way, it was Friday. It was girl's night and she was just going to hang with her buds and pretend that Wednesday night hadn't happened.

"Oh, you started without us," Kate said, flicking her long red ponytail over one shoulder. "What's wrong?"

Cora took one look at Kelsey's face and knew. Cora had been her closest friend since elementary school and even though they'd only been in the same grade for one year before Kels had started skipping grades, they'd remained close. She was also the only person in the universe who knew about Tanner.

Heidi, meanwhile, was studying Kelsey closely. "No book,

even on book club night. Beer in hand, even though she only normally tolerates it because we like beer. Hollow look in her eyes—"

Kels smacked her. "Stop. My eyes are *not* hollow."

Cora plunked down into the booth next to her. "They kind of are." Her book smacked on the table. "Let's forget talking about this. It sucked, and I only read the summary online anyway."

"Cora!" Kate said. "How could you?"

Heidi narrowed her eyes. "We have one rule for book club. You read the book or—" She made a slicing motion across her throat.

That, at least, made Kels smile. "Since when?"

"Since we stopped reading all the books we were *supposed*"—she made air quotes here—"to be reading and just started going for the ones we wanted to read."

"Well then, what happened with this month?" Cora asked, pouring herself a beer. "Admit it, none of us wanted to read it."

She looked at Kels, who nodded and shrugged. "It's true."

Heidi winced.

Kate gasped. "I thought you guys were into—"

"The existential crisis of the white man?" Cora said. "Not so much. Especially when the first half is about how difficult their lives are."

"It's difficult having all that power," Heidi muttered.

"It was at the top of the bestseller's list and—"

Cora gasped. "You didn't read it either! You bitch!"

Kate bit her lip, cheeks turning pink. "No," she admitted. "Honestly, I suggested it as a joke and couldn't believe you guys agreed to it."

Heidi smacked her. "I spent fifteen bucks on the ebook! *Fifteen!* What the hell!"

Kelsey snorted.

Her friends looked at her, Cora beyond affronted, Kate blushing though her expression was quietly mischievous, and Heidi's eyes sparking with frustration.

"I love you guys," she said and felt a tear streak down her cheek.

The book by a well-known asshole, albeit a damned good prank on quiet Kate's part, was forgotten and her friends all began talking at once.

"Tears, Kels? Holy shit, did you get fired?" Heidi.

"Is your family okay?" Kate.

"Tanner." Cora.

She sucked in a shuddering breath and released it, dashing the tear away and thankful that one of the very few social things she'd learned during her time in college was how to put on makeup that stayed. The older girls had thrown her a solid. Big time. Big—

"Kelsey!"

She blinked and stepped back on the conversational road. "Sorry," she murmured. "Family is fine. Great actually. Devon and Becca had their baby, and I'm going shopping with Rachel soon for stuff to wear on her honeymoon. Work is busy but good."

"Which leaves Tanner," Cora said.

"Who's Tanner?" Kate asked.

Kelsey didn't know where to begin, but as usual, Cora had her covered. She shoved the book aside and filled Heidi and Kate's glasses. "Tanner is Bas's friend, and Kels has been in love with him for her entire existence."

"Not entire," she muttered.

"Okay, since she was eight years old and Tanner helped her get a Band-Aid or something."

"It was a Band-Aid *and* ice," Kelsey corrected. "And my mom."

"Aw," Kate murmured.

"How come we've never heard about Tanner?" Heidi asked.

"There was no point," Kels said. "We were together one summer, for a couple of months. He dumped me and left the country and hasn't been back for nine years."

"But we've been friends for nine years," Heidi protested.

"Part of the reason I went back for my post-doc was because of him. I needed something to fill my time."

Cora rolled her eyes. "Only you would consider getting a PhD as something to fill your time outside of a normal forty-hour workweek."

"Well," Kate said, reaching across the booth and squeezing Kels's hand. "Whatever reason you went back to school, I'm glad you ended up in my path." She smiled. "I got a good friend out of it."

Cora rolled her eyes again. "Stop being sappy," she snapped. "You're making us look bad."

"You're the worst," Kate snapped.

Heidi sighed. "Can we focus on why Tanner and Kelsey only lasted a few months?"

Kels shrugged. "Things were good, or so I thought. Inseparable for almost the whole summer, but then adulthood was calling, and my job had started, and I wanted us to tell my family. At first, sneaking around was fun, but eventually I wanted us to just be a real couple, you know?"

"Seems reasonable," Kate said.

"I thought so, too, and I thought he was on board. I suggested it, he agreed, but then the next day he called and broke up with me." Kels took a sip of her beer. "Then he left the country and didn't come back."

"For how long?" Heidi asked.

"He came back two days ago because he's in Bas's wedding.

Apparently, he's been keeping touch with my brother but not me."

"Well, he was Bas's friend first," Cora said. "It makes sense that they'd stay friends."

"That's it!" Kate exclaimed.

"What?"

"He must be hung up on the fact that Bas is your brother."

"That's stupid," Kelsey said.

Cora considered for a moment. "Stupid on his part, yes, but it is feasible. Men get stupid when it comes to sisters."

Considering that Cora had six brothers, Kelsey figured she understood the concept well. And she supposed it could be true, though she'd never considered the fact that the reason Tan had left was because of his relationship with her brothers. Given Bas's tendency towards aloofness when he'd been younger, she'd always just figured Tanner's interest had been there, but he'd waited until she was old enough. He and Devon had been close, too, but Dev was older and not home much. He'd been as engaged as he could be, of course. Just as a professional athlete, he hadn't had a ton of time for her or the rest of the family.

But Tanner had. He *always* had.

He'd been at her house sometimes more frequently than her own brothers.

She'd always figured that was because of her. But what if it hadn't been? What if he only wanted her because of her family?

She groaned and plunked her head on the table.

"What?" Cora asked.

"He's an only child. His parents are shit. Mine basically took him in when he was in middle school."

"Oh," Kate and Heidi said, though this wasn't news to Cora.

"He didn't have something to lose if things went wrong with you, Kels," she said. "He had it *all* to lose."

Kelsey glared up at Cora. "Why didn't you ever say anything?"

Cora put her hands up in surrender. "We were eighteen. I didn't exactly have a wealth of experience with boys back then."

True. Considering she was the youngest of six very protective brothers and her dad had passed shortly after she'd been born, that was *exceptionally* true. Cora had barely been allowed to go to prom, and that was only because Kelsey had gone as her date. Her brothers continued to meddle in her life to this day.

"Sorry," she said, bumping Cora's shoulder with her own.

"Not offended. But now that we all know what happened in the past, it's time to talk about the present."

She wrinkled her nose. "Technically what happened with Tanner was two days ago, so that is the past, too, and I'd just as soon pretend it never happened."

Heidi pfted. "In what world do you think we'd let you get away with that?"

Kels turned sad eyes to Kate, but even her sweet friend didn't soften. "Dish," she said. "Now."

"Ugh. Guys!" Kels's cheeks got hot just thinking about what had happened. "It's so embarrassing."

"More than me puking on my boss's shoes?" Kate asked.

"Yes."

"How about me having two too many beers and then puking on the hot, tattooed bartender?" Heidi asked.

"Yes," Kels snapped. "And you're lucky he let you back in here. Bobby's is the shit, and it would suck infinitely to have to find a new place to hang out."

"I bought him an entire new outfit," she admitted, "and promised to only have one beer a night for the rest of my time in Bobby's." They all glanced toward the bar, where sexy as sin, Kace, reigned supreme. He lifted a brow, lips curving the slightest bit, but then he returned his attention to his work.

Though, Kels watched a little longer, maybe he was pretending to work because—

"He's got a thing for the redhead working in the corner," Cora murmured. "Wouldn't have thought she was his type."

"Lucky girl," Kate said.

Heidi just sighed, and it was all jealous.

Kelsey knew the feeling, though she thought sun-kissed photojournalists were more her speed. She picked up her cell. "Oops," she said. "I forgot I have a conference call in the morning. I should—"

"Don't get distracted, girls," Cora declared. "She's trying to give us the slip."

Kate shook her head. "Tomorrow is Saturday, babe. Even you don't work on Saturdays."

"I—"

Heidi pointed a finger at her. "You. Share your embarrassing tale of woe now or so help me, God, I'll make next month's book an autobiography."

Kels shuddered.

"I'll do it," Heidi pressed.

She would and since it was her month to pick, they all had to shut up and take it. *Ugh.* What a metaphor in a time like this. When all *she'd* wanted to do was shut up and take it from Tan. But that wasn't happening.

"Fine," she said and began detailing the entire sordid tale. By the time she got to the point of taking off her bra and stepping out of her panties, her friends were gaping at her. "Then I walked into the bedroom, expecting him to come right after me."

Cora's voice was quiet. "He didn't?"

"No." Kels's eyes prickled again. "I waited and then I heard the door shut. When I peeked back in the hallway, he was gone."

"Oh shit," Kate said.

"Yeah." She pressed her hands to her cheeks. "The thought of seeing him again, after him just leaving . . . I don't know how to cope with that."

"Not to be an asshole," Cora said. "But, for Bas's sake, you're going to have to figure out a way."

Kels groaned. "I know." She plunked her head back down onto the table. "So, what's the play? I pretend nothing happened?"

"Hell no." Cora.

"Yes." Kate.

"Yes *and* no." Heidi.

Kelsey looked up at her friend. "Explain yourself."

"From what I've heard, it sounds as though Tanner really likes you—"

She snorted, disbelieving.

"He wouldn't have kissed you if he didn't like you," Heidi pointed out. "And he kissed you first, so that's big. It means he's into you, even if he doesn't want to be."

"Great. Ringing endorsement." She leaned back in the booth and crossed her arms. Into her even though he doesn't want to be. Perfect. Such a confidence booster.

"Shut up and listen," Kate said, and that snapped her out of her pity party, because Kate wasn't tough and rarely lost her cool. If she was telling Kelsey to focus, she should do just that.

"It's the typical tortured hero," Heidi said, speaking of one of their favorite romance tropes. "Tough past. Scared of bringing that into the future, so he either lashes out to push the heroine away *or* he does everything in his power to keep his distance." She picked up her glass and took a large swallow, looking awfully proud of herself.

As she should be.

Kels sat up straight.

"He did both," she said, stunned. "Pushed me away and ran."

"And this time he ran again," Cora said. "So the pushing away might be coming next."

Fuck. "That's true."

"What you need to decide," Kate said, "is if he's worth trying to force your way through the barricades and fire he's going to put in your path."

"And," Heidi said. "This isn't a book. It's real-life. Happy endings aren't guaranteed. Which means you may put yourself out there and not get the guy in the end."

Kels traced her finger along the outside of her glass. "You all are sure building my confidence tonight."

"If you wanted confidence building, you wouldn't be friends with us," Cora said. "We love you, but we always give it to each other straight. No bullshit."

Kelsey sighed. "So basically, I need to decide if pursuing things with Tanner is worth my potentially getting my heart stomped on again."

"Or run over by a train." Kate

"Or put through a blender and making a heartbreak smoothie." Heidi.

"Or having your ass hanging out there where none of us can do a damned thing to protect it from getting spanked." Cora.

"Cruel, but true," she said to Kate. "Gross." To Heidi. "And thanks for putting it in that particularly poetic way." Cora. She sighed, finished off her beer then picked up her glass of water. "Now, can we please talk about something else aside from my embarrassing as shit naked exploits?"

"How about we talk about that time you got locked out of your apartment with three gallons of ice cream and tried to eat them all so they wouldn't melt while you waited for the super?" Cora put in helpfully.

Kels shook her head, but she was smiling. "You guys really are the worst."

"And if by worst, you mean the *best*, then yes."

Thankfully, Kate took pity on her and changed the subject to *Outlander*—which Kels was now caught up on, thanks to the all-nighter she'd pulled after Tanner's escape act on Wednesday —and they spent the next few hours discussing all the merits of Jamie and Claire and how the show compared to the books thus far.

Getting lost in the fictional world of her favorite highlander meant that by the time they were walking out of Bobby's, Kelsey felt much more like herself again.

Or at least she wasn't going to expire of embarrassment.

She said goodbye to her friends then drove back into the City and to her apartment, but the quiet of the road brought everything back into the forefront of her mind again.

Tanner was her weak spot. He always had been.

And she'd demonstrated that fact quite clearly—cough, *painfully*—after he'd been back in town for only a few hours.

Her hands tightened on the steering wheel. Fucking pathetic.

Her. Him. The whole situation.

This wasn't a fairy tale. She couldn't fix him. And frankly . . . she didn't want to have that kind of responsibility. She'd been destroyed by his issues once, and that was more than enough. Or maybe it was less that he had issues and more that he didn't want her. Or want her enough to deal with the flack that was sure to come from her brothers.

That thought was almost as painful as the embarrassment she'd felt from his leaving her naked and wanting.

It also reinforced the fact that she needed to get her head on straight, to keep her heart safe.

And to make a commitment to never get naked in front of Tanner Pearson again.

Decision made.

Her ass would be staying safely in her pants from here on out.

EIGHT

Tanner

HE WOKE WITH A START, hard and aching and sweating, his cock about two seconds from exploding all over his stomach.

A wet dream.

About Kelsey.

It wouldn't be the first time he'd had one.

Or even the first one this month.

But it was the first time he'd had one and hadn't woken up without at least having finished. Embarrassingly, he was disappointed by that fact, disappointed that he couldn't share an orgasm with Kelsey, even in his dreams.

"Shit," he muttered, and because it was four in the morning, because he was jet-lagged and throbbing, he gripped the length of his erection and started stroking. Pink-tipped nipples, turquoise lace, lips that had parted the moment his had touched hers, a tongue that wasn't shy as it had stroked against his. Long legs around his hips, hands in his hair, a husky moan in the back of her throat—

He came for a long time, cock pulsing, spine bowing, sweat dripping down his temples into his hair.

"Fuck."

Tanner reached over to the nightstand and grabbed the box of tissues he'd started keeping there. Like a fucking teenager. Christ, next thing he knew, and he'd be keeping some lotion there as well. To prevent chafing.

Cute.

Sighing, he pushed out of bed.

The jet lag was getting better, even if he was up at 4:16 in the morning. He was used to early mornings, used to getting up before the sun rose and getting into position to capture the best light.

But there wasn't a reason to get up anymore.

He'd stopped taking new contracts a year ago, had told his agent to no longer send him queries because he was taking an indefinite break.

Something Tom wasn't the least bit happy about since he got a percentage of every contract. But Tan didn't give a shit at this point. He'd worked his way up from taking photos at family and friends' events to traveling on a shoestring budget, picking something that struck him as compelling to capture then hoping like hell he might find someone who might want to buy his photographs. Eventually, he'd landed Tom and become in high demand for nature magazines. But after a portrait he'd snapped of a friend of a friend—who'd turned out to be a famous celebrity he didn't know because he spent most of his life away from the Internet—he'd been asked to take photos for various industry events and high fashion magazines.

He'd done it all.

Because he'd been hungry to prove himself.

But also because he'd been motivated to forget.

Then Kelsey had called him.

It had all begun unraveling then. He'd started dreaming of her at eighteen, of their time together—and not just sex dreams because he wasn't a total pervert. He'd remembered curling up on the couch, sharing a bowl of popcorn and laughing like loons at some comedy he probably wouldn't find funny nowadays. He remembered the way her smile used to change, just minutely, when she met his eyes, as though she held him in a special place in her heart.

And he remembered what he'd said to her to push her away.

The way her breathing had hitched when he'd wounded her.

For years he'd tried to forget it all, to bury it in work.

And a thirty-second phone call had made him realize how absolutely useless all the years of hiding had been. He'd never been able to get her out of his heart or brain. He had the feeling he never would.

Suddenly the fast-paced cities he was photographing in Asia had seemed dull, the beautiful beaches and ocean uninspired, the people faceless. Tan had gotten the necessary shots, had done his job because he was a fucking professional, but he'd hated every single moment of it.

Then he'd come home.

Or back to the states, at least.

Back to Kelsey.

But nothing had changed.

She felt like home, was captivating and brilliant and gorgeous. Still tempted him like no other woman ever had, and she still had the ability to burrow deep into his soul. Yet, *nothing* had changed. He was broken inside, so what could he possibly offer her?

He ran when things got tough.

His parents hadn't even wanted him.

All he could give Kelsey was an uncertain future and one half of a man.

The urge to hit the road and find whatever means necessary to disappear was intense, and the only thing that was stopping him from bolting was Sebastian. He might be a dick and screw-up, but the last thing he was going to do was fuck up his friend's wedding.

Tanner also knew that even if he ran again, even if he took all the jobs Tom wanted him to, that he'd never be able to shake off the feel of Kelsey in his arms.

Before he'd relegated the memories to the back of his mind, tucked safely away.

Now they were out and just like Pandora's Box, there was no going back to the way things were.

Sighing, he buried the tissues in the garbage can, took a quick shower and dressed, then grabbed his backpack and went down to the lobby. It was habit to check his bag for his camera, along with additional batteries and a handful of extra memory cards—a photographer never wanted to run out of disk space or for their camera to die mid-shoot.

Outside the sky was dark and the morning commute was just beginning, lines of lights trailing through the street, white coming toward him, turning red as they passed, but he could see just the barest glimmer of sunlight in the East.

As he walked, he'd pause at whatever struck his fancy and take a shot. With the changing lights and traffic building, it was a lesson in balancing technique with his artistic presence. But really, he was just playing around, pointing his camera in any direction, even purposefully ruining some pictures with too much light or not enough focus.

Sometimes good things happened when he broke the rules.

His camera had been pointed at the dark silhouette of a gothic building against the lightening sky when he'd had that thought, but the moment it crossed his brain, his lens drooped, and he ended up getting a shot of a pigeon's head peeking around the eaves.

See what he meant about good things?

But he couldn't appreciate the irony of that statement when he was shocked senseless by what he'd just thought.

When he broke the rules in his work, good things happened.

So why was he so terrified of breaking the rules where Kelsey was concerned?

He lifted his camera and hit the button, capturing the shot he'd imagined before, but it was even better than he'd thought it would be because he shot a little later, because there was more light available, and—

He was terrified of breaking the rules because Kelsey was so much more important than a picture. Quite simply, the stakes were higher.

But, with that piece of information straight in his head, he continued moving, kept doing his best to fill those memory cards, and by the time the sun was high in the sky, he'd found some of the happy that being behind the lens used to give him. The world focused to just a small circle, one that he could control and move as he saw fit. Tan was king of that lensed world, even if his subjects occasionally got a little squirrely and uncooperative.

Eventually, his arms got tired, his eyes tired, and his empty memory card supply dangerously low, so he decided to head back to the hotel.

Since he'd been wandering for hours without paying much attention to directions or landmarks, he pulled out his cell and spent a few minutes with the map to plot his course home. Then he started walking, larger intersections transforming into smaller twisting streets and nicer apartments.

A flash of green caught his attention just as he turned the street corner, and for a moment his breath caught in his lungs.

So fucking beautiful.

Fog hugging the ground, the sun having burned away the pockets overhead, but this little enclave of green was shadowed by the buildings surrounding it, and so the fog lived on, curling mist that garnished silver and black stones.

A cemetery perhaps wasn't the most obvious choice for beauty, but this one was.

Or perhaps it was the man kneeling over a flat headstone, brushing away the leaves and dirt before placing a bouquet of yellow daffodils on its surface.

Tan lifted his camera to capture the moment—sun drifting through the fog, highlighting the yellow flowers, silhouetting the man against the gray mist, the green grass bright, the black and white of the other headstones making the entire image otherworldly.

The *click* of the shutter startled him.

He dropped his camera, realized he was intruding on a private moment.

Shit.

As painful as it was, he'd delete the image when he got back to the hotel.

"Don't."

The raspy voice startled Tan, and he glanced up to see that the old man had made his way over to him, beige jacket darkened in speckles where the moisture had clung to the air.

"I'm sorry," Tan said. "I'll delete the photograph. Usually I ask before I shoot, I was just so taken by the moment . . ." He cleared his throat. "It was beautiful."

Pale brown eyes studied him for a long moment then the man pushed open the gate to the small cemetery. "Come."

Tan bit his tongue, swallowed his questions, and followed the man through the path to the grave he'd been kneeling at.

Rosario Hernadez, Loving Wife and Mother.

"My Rosie was beautiful," the man said softly.

"Were daffodils her favorite?" Tan asked.

A nod. "She'd get the biggest smile on her face when I'd bring them to her." His voice went sad. "I'd give anything to see that again."

The dates on the headstone told Tanner that the loss had been recent, and he found himself clasping the man's shoulder. "Did you have a lot of years together?"

Tears glittered, but the man nodded. "We did. Almost fifty, and yet it seems to have gone by in a flash."

"What were some things you loved about her?"

He smiled. "My Rosie was very competitive. Never met a board game she didn't have to win." Mischief crept into his expression. "Or an argument. She always made sure I had the type of drinks I loved, only cooked the meals I hated when I really made her mad."

Tan laughed.

"And she gave me a beautiful family. A beautiful life."

The tears were still in the man's eyes, but there was also something else—peace. Relief in knowing that even if the time spent with the woman he loved was ephemeral, he still held tight to those memories, those emotions.

"I wanted forever," the man said. "Even knowing that wasn't possible. And now that I find myself without forever, I still know I wouldn't change a single day."

Nothing was permanent.

Tanner lifted the camera without thinking, capturing the love on the man's face, how even though his heart was shattered because the incredible thing he'd had was now gone, he still understood he'd had something precious, and that precious thing was to be protected.

The man blinked, glanced at the camera.

"Sorry," Tanner said. "I—" He shook his head. "I'll delete them."

A warm hand stayed his when he began fumbling with his camera. "Don't." Then the old man reached into his pocket and pulled out a card. "Will you send them to me?"

Tan held his breath for a long moment, then carefully pocketed the card. "Yes."

"Good man," he said and turned back to the headstone.

"Would you—" Pale brown eyes found his again, warmer this time, and that gave Tan the strength to finish the question. "Would you do it again?"

The man opened his mouth to reply, but Tanner pressed on because that wasn't quite the question he'd wanted to ask. "I mean, if you knew you were going to screw things up, that there was no way that you could keep Rosie forever because you weren't good enough for her, couldn't give her everything she wanted . . . would you still go for it?"

The man was quiet for a long time.

Then he said, "Yes."

And that was it.

Tanner swallowed hard and nodded.

"You're going to screw up," he said when Tan started to turn away. "There are going to be times when everything you have to give her isn't enough. Life isn't fair or easy. It takes courage. Courage to leap and grab hold. Courage to hope that you'll be able to figure out what *is* enough." He pointed at Rosie's headstone. "Together."

The man bent and swept off one last leaf then squeezed Tan's arm as he left.

Tanner didn't know how long he stood there, staring off in to space, processing the words the man had said, feeling them shift all the pieces in his mind and heart around until they all started to make sense.

Maybe he *could* be enough.

His cell buzzed, jolting him out of reverie. He left the cemetery, turning back in the direction of the hotel, and he pulled it out of his pocket to see that Bas had sent him a text inviting him to dinner at his parents' place that night. With all three of their kids in the Bay Area, the Scotts had sold their house in the Midwest and moved to a town east of San Francisco.

It was smaller than the home they'd raised their kids in and supposedly quite a heap, according to Devon. But Grant had recently retired and wanted a project to keep him busy.

Or maybe it was more accurate to say that Megan, who'd quit her job as a classroom aid when they'd moved and whom Grant was driving absolutely crazy, had wanted to give him a project.

At least, this was all according to Bas.

But the Scotts were a close-knit family, and Tanner figured it was accurate gossip.

Poor Megan had probably imagined California as all sunny beaches, fruity cocktails, and avocado toast, but as most people who made it to the northern part of the Golden State eventually discovered, the north and south were vastly different. The southern part had the warm beaches, while the northern part had the frigid, only-swimmable-if-someone-was-crazy ocean. Cocktails were more likely to be wine, though avocado toast *was* prevalent.

He made a mental note to buy Megan and Grant a trip to Hawaii for Christmas that year then typed out a quick response to Bas saying he'd be there.

To which Bas replied:

Great. Want to get a ride with Kelsey? She's driving over.

The universe hated him.

Kels okay with that?

Which was really fucking unlikely given the way he'd left her on Wednesday night.

Of course, she'll be. I'll send her a text.

Oh, for fuck's sake.

I've got her number. I'll make sure it's not an inconvenience.

A few seconds passed.

Why do you have her number?

He cursed, pushed his way into the lobby and considered telling his best friend that he'd spent a summer boning his sister and then the nine years since imagining doing it in all the ways his twenty-one-year-old self had been too uninspired to think of at the time. Probably unwise. Snorting, he sent something safer.

Dude, I have every Scott's number. It's an occupational hazard of being practically adopted into the family.

Then.

Heading into an elevator. Will see you tonight.

As the floors sped by, he considered his options. One, he could ignore Bas's suggestion and take BART—the local public transit—to the east bay. This might be the safest option—well, not safe in terms of potential for bodily harm, but safe because he wouldn't be in close proximity to Kels. However, there were some sketchy stations if Bas was to be believed, and then there would be an explanation required for why he didn't actually ask for a ride. Second, he could ask Kelsey for the ride and risk her running him over in the parking lot of her building. Third—

Third . . . he could give up the fight, accept that it was impossible to keep Kelsey at a distance, and just go for what the universe had been telling him.

Third was the scariest.

NINE

Kelsey

HER PHONE BUZZED when she was mid-bite, and the contents of the text message made her oatmeal slop off her spoon and onto the table.

"Are you fucking kidding me?" she hissed, dropping the utensil into the bowl and trying to resist the urge to launch her cell across the room. She'd committed to forgetting Tanner, to closing up her heart and moving on from Tanner.

And now he was texting her, asking her to voluntarily spend the equivalent of two hours trapped in a car with him.

She plunked the phone on the counter then picked up her bowl.

"Stupid *fucking* men." She set the half-full bowl in the sink. Set, not tossed because she'd gotten her dinnerware at a really kitschy store that was no longer in business. The pieces were hand-thrown, each one a little different and all glazed in irides-cent blue. Kels had loved the way they were edged, loved how the slight wave reminded her of a flower.

She'd bought a full set of twelve bowls, dinner plates, and

salad plates, and since she hosted meals at her house exactly *never,* that hadn't been an efficient use of her funds *or* cabinet space.

Still, she'd loved them, so she'd bought them then had dealt with the fallout of sacrificing an entire kitchen cabinet to store them.

Sometimes in life a woman had to make sacrifices.

Snorting, she filled the bowl with water before turning to rest her hips against the lip of the counter.

One day and her resolve to keep her distance from Tanner was kaput. Because, frankly, there was more than one type of distance. Emotional as well as physical, and riding in a car with him was about as far from keeping her physically away from Tan as possible. Then there was her reaction to his request.

Joy.

Excitement to be in his presence.

And then fury because she was such a fucking idiot. If he'd wanted something more than friendship from her, he would have taken it on Wednesday night. Even if he'd thought they were rushing things or that they should slow down and take a breath, he would have made it clear that he was leaving because of that and not disappeared out the door like a freaking ninja.

Seriously, if it hadn't been for her trail of underthings, she could have almost pretended she'd been hallucinating.

But the trail had been there, and her embarrassment was undying, and—

No, she couldn't be trapped in a car with him for two-plus hours!

So she texted him back.

Sorry. Can't.

Lame, but it saved her, and that was what she needed.

Setting her phone on the table, she started for the shower. She'd slept in that morning, watched a few new episodes of *Killing Eve,* then had subjected herself to an hour of Pilates.

Now it was lunchtime and she'd lost her appetite for her oatmeal, which conveniently was the only semi-palatable food she had left in her house. Maybe she'd treat herself to Molly's. They made the most incredible pear and walnut salad, and they probably had their new soups of the day out.

Yes. That was the perfect plan.

Drown her sorrows in raspberry vinaigrette and candied walnuts—

Buzz buzz.

How about a ride home then?

Ugh. She snagged her cell and headed for the bathroom, starting up the shower and debating what to say.

In the end, she settled on,

Sorry. No.

She wasn't sorry, but it definitely was a no, and so she left it at that and put the phone down again. By then the shower was warm, so she stripped off her sweaty clothes. The hot water hitting her skin was everything she needed in her life, sluicing down her hair, warming her from the outside in.

It soothed the muscles she'd tortured during her workout, and it also effectively blocked any noise of her cell's potential vibration.

Eventually, she'd pruned herself up enough and turned off the water.

No sooner had she toweled off, then her eyes found her cell.

Sure enough, a text was on the screen.

*Understood. But you're going to have to think up a reason
to tell Bas why you're not available to drive me when he
knows you are coming to dinner and already offered you
up as a ride option.*

"Shit," she muttered.

He was right, of course, Bas had called her earlier that day,
asked her what she was doing, and like an imbecile, she'd dished
about her plans to do nothing but veg out before going to the
family dinner.

Maybe she could think of some excuse at work?

Wait. Damn, that wouldn't work. Not so long as she and Bas
were working on the joint RoboTech/Steele Technologies
project. If she lied and said there was an issue with the product
that she had to go into work to deal with, but didn't tell him
immediately, he'd be beyond pissed.

Yes, they were siblings, but they were also partners on this
product, and RoboTech didn't screw over their partners—or
leave them out of the loop on potential problems, fake or
otherwise.

Not to mention that lying about the project would quite
possibly get her fired, and she really liked her job.

So work was out.

Maybe she could fake the sudden onset of the flu?

Bas wouldn't buy it.

An existential crisis that required her to stay in and gorge on
Oreos she'd ordered in on InstaCart?

Ick.

There was a reason that she tended to lack a filter. She
didn't like lying, and while yes, she had to admit that lying
wasn't a skill she'd managed to hone over the years, she also
didn't like lying because it made her feel bad inside.

Usually, she just gave her answer with as little of the negative details as possible.

Hence, *Sorry. No.*

So she either—

And dammit, she flung her cell onto the bed and stormed to the closet, thinking that her life over the last few days had been filled with way too many *eithers* and ultimatums.

She either drove him or lied.

She either offered her heart up to potentially be shredded by Tanner or she let him go.

She either put aside how much he'd hurt her nine years ago or she ruined her brother's wedding.

She either sucked it up and pretended everything was fine . . . or—

What else could she do?

Kelsey had had plenty of experience with pretending things were fine.

This would be just another day. Her fingers moved across her cell's screen.

Be in the lobby by four.

THANK God for Molly's and their perfectly caramelized walnuts.

Those nuts in her mouth were the only thing getting her through this day—yes, insert snort there—but the point was that Molly's fabulous salad was distracting her from what was coming in T-minus one hour.

Sighing, she closed her paperback and started gathering her things.

She needed to change before Tanner showed up, to put

herself together in a way that would allow her mom to miss that she was falling apart inside.

Though, with the wedding rapidly approaching and Devon's baby newly born into the world and altogether adorable, Kels's mom was missing plenty these days.

Still, she didn't need to slip up and get on the radar.

These were dark, dark days.

Potential motherly intervention before, during (or truthfully, *after*) Bas's long-awaited wedding—complete with the giant cake and seat covers and white poofy dress—wasn't something Kelsey wanted to deal with.

And more importantly, she wasn't going to mess up a single detail of her brother's big day.

Bas had waited a long time to be happy, and Rachel had been put through the wringer. Rachel's ex-husband was—or had been—a creep of the worst kind. He'd abused her repeatedly then had come after her in California when she'd tried to divorce him. Plus, her mom had left, her father was cruel and mostly absentee, and her grandparents, who'd basically raised her, had treated her like garbage. Things had worked out in the end, but Rachel had suffered in the process, spending a good deal of her life trying to escape her past.

Hmm. Kind of like Tanner and his escape act.

Not that his childhood was anything when compared to Rachel's, but he'd been obviously neglected and not a priority to his parents in the least. That had to leave scars.

Kels wondered if that was a Scott family trait, finding partners that were wounded and needed rescuing.

It wasn't like their lives growing up had been bump free or all sunshine and rainbows, but they'd had two parents who'd loved them, a steady home, food on the table. That was a lot more than most.

But also maybe that made her and her brothers choose lovers who hadn't had it as good.

Share the wealth of good.

She snorted.

Might as well don a crown and hold a fairy princess wand. She didn't wield that sort of power, couldn't change someone or make their past better. She was just a girl, living her life, and trying not to fuck up too much.

Still, it did bear some pondering, that Scott tendency to rescue.

Dev had rescued his wife, Becca. Or at least, he'd helped her out when she'd been in a tough spot and quite literally had protected her from some creep who'd been trying to hurt her.

Bas had rescued Rachel, though she'd resent the term and say the rescuing was mutual. Which it was. But according to Heather, Rachel's boss, Rach had been shut down and scared and hurting, with Sebastian as the only one to penetrate those layers of heavy, steel armor around her heart.

And Tanner.

When she was eighteen, she'd thought she might be enough to fill that hole inside him.

But in dramatic, teenage-broken-heart fashion, she'd been proven wrong.

Painfully wrong.

Ugh.

Enough.

She shoved her book into her purse, left a tip on the table, and bustled out of the restaurant. Twenty minutes later, she'd swapped her comfy leggings for jeans, her sneakers for flats, her scarf for a jumble of necklaces.

No primping.

As in, she wasn't going to allow herself to put any more effort into her appearance than she normally would for a visit to her parents' by resisting the urge to glam it up and shove in Tanner's nose exactly what he'd been missing out on Wednesday.

But she'd already shown him everything, and look how that had turned out.

So instead, Kels did the bare minimum, made sure she had a playlist on her phone—no way was she making the mistake of not filling the silence in her car this time. Then she grabbed her purse, jacket, and keys and headed for the door.

The knock greeted her just as she arrived.

"Fuck," she muttered, having no idea that Tanner was saying the exact same thing on the other side of the door.

TEN

Tanner

"FUCK," Tanner muttered after he'd knocked, trying to resist the urge to shove his hand through his hair.

He was equal parts convinced this was the stupidest thing he'd ever done and also maybe the smartest.

Kelsey was—

The door opened, and his breath caught.

Absolutely beautiful.

He could almost imagine that this was a real date, that he hadn't fucked her over twice and that they were making a real go of this.

If she hadn't looked like she wanted to kill him.

Blue eyes sparked with annoyance, and Tan was probably kidding himself, but he could have sworn there was a trace of heat in her expression. If it *had* been present and not a figment of his imagination, then it was gone in a millisecond, a tight mask of annoyance locked in place over her face.

Still beautiful, even when furious.

She didn't say anything, just stepped out, closed and locked the door, then headed for the elevator.

"Hi," he said.

Nothing.

"Good talk," he couldn't resist saying.

Kels spun around so fast that her ponytail smacked her in the face. "What did you say?"

He caught the ends and rubbed them between his fingers, and fuck, that simple touch was enough for him to *remember*.

Hairs tangling over his face as she slept sprawled across his chest, tendrils escaping her ponytail as she'd sat across the table from him working on some multiple-page proof, long strands damp from the shower and smelling like roses.

Roses she still smelled like.

Kelsey jumped back, wrenching her hair from his fingers, the ends catching in a way that had to be painful. Her wince of discomfort made him feel like even more of a shitbag.

"Don't touch," she snapped, wrenching back around in a way that made *him* wince, or at the very least, worry for her spine.

Yet, even furious, she was still the most beautiful thing he'd ever seen.

And for a man like him, one who'd seen more breathtaking landmarks in just a few years than people saw in their entire lifetimes, that wasn't easy to do.

It wasn't bullshit either.

Her brown eyes rivaled the desert sand of the Sahara, her hair as lush and thick as the foliage in the jungles of the Amazon. Kels's skin was softer than the merino wool he'd touched in New Zealand, her scent more delicate than the roses he'd photographed in the Queen's garden in England. She was . . . well, putting aside his pathetic rambling, Kelsey had always been with him.

As he'd gone through his memory cards, deleting most of what he'd shot, only saving the couple that might be good enough for publication—even though he was technically retired, old habits died hard. But then as he had studied the photographs from the cemetery, witnessing the love and devotion on the man's face all over again, feeling those same emotions pulse in his heart when he thought of Kelsey, Tan had come to the realization that no matter how far he'd traveled, she had always been in his heart.

So, he'd decided to go with option three.

He was going to keep her.

The thought of fucking things up with her still terrified him. He didn't know how to do something good, but he also didn't know how to be in this world and not have Kelsey. And he'd take on any of the Scotts who had a problem with that, whether it was Devon or Sebastian or Grant or Megan. He'd prove to them that he could make her happy.

He just had to figure out how to convince Kels to let him.

Figures, he'd already dug himself a giant hole in that department.

Back stiff as a board, she jabbed at the elevator button. Repeatedly.

Tan held on to his hope. The no touching thing, the irritation in his presence, the purposeful ignoring . . . all of those were good things. Well, not *good* exactly, because he'd prefer to go back to Wednesday and make a different choice, but those emotions also meant Kelsey was still feeling something for him.

Annoyance was just a hairsbreadth away from makeup sex.

Yeah, sure it was. But makeup sex or not, she felt something, and so that meant he wasn't going to give up.

Of course, annoyance was also very close to dead-to-her, and so Tanner needed to make sure he didn't fuck things up further.

Internally sighing, he followed Kels to the elevator, purposefully standing very close, but also not touching. Yes, he was an asshole. Yes, he planned on pushing that very boundary. No, he wouldn't cross the line she'd drawn without her asking him to. Still, that didn't mean he couldn't soak up as much of her as possible, starting with the scent that had been imprinted on his senses.

"Did you just *sniff* me?" She turned slightly, ponytail whipping around again, though this time it slapped *him* in the cheek.

Play it cool.

"Hmm?" he asked.

"Did you—"

The elevator doors opened with a ding, and Tan hurried in front of Kels, partly to ensure the metal panels didn't close on her, but mostly to avoid having to answer her question.

He pressed the button for the garage. "You coming?"

Her nose wrinkled, but she stepped onto the elevator, positioning herself with her back to the corner.

The one furthest from him.

Yeah. She felt something. He just had to convince her doing something about that *something* was worth it.

They rode down to the garage in silence, but she surprised him by handing over the keys as they approached her car. "I can't stand driving," she told him. "And you might as well make yourself useful."

"Putting me to work?"

"I should put you *somewhere*," she muttered, plunking herself down in the passenger's side and reaching for the seat belt.

He beat her to it, grabbing the buckle and stretching it over her lap. Her breath hitched and because he'd purposefully put himself as close as possible without actually touching, he felt those warm puffs of air on his neck.

Hot. Damp.

Fuck.

Now he *felt* it somewhere else.

He closed his eyes, struggling to call up some control. Him taking option three (his keeping Kelsey . . . permanently) didn't mean he could just waltz back into her life and fuck it up more than he'd already done. He needed to move slow, to move with caution. To show her he knew he'd fucked up, but that he wasn't going to do it again.

To prove that he wasn't going to hurt her again.

Kissing her senseless and then tossing her in the backseat to ravage her like a teenager on prom night wouldn't prove anything.

So he sucked in a breath, braced himself against the dizziness that came from having so much of her intoxicating scent in his nose, and buckled her seat belt.

The *click* was gunshot loud in the quiet garage.

Tanner blinked, started to shake his head to clear it.

Fingers in his hair, along his jaw.

He shuddered. The hand on his face shook.

His eyes swung to the side, saw her brown ones were clouded with desire. Lush, pink lips parted. "Tan—"

A car alarm went off, making them both jump.

Then the fingers slipped away, tucked back into the safety of Kelsey's lap. He shifted, straightening out of her sedan, and trying to remember that he was *not* going to ravish her in the backseat.

Swallowing, he retreated a step and closed the car door.

He'd been looking forward to the drive initially, thinking it would be a good start to him proving himself.

Now he was thinking that two-plus hours trapped in a metal box with Kelsey was going to be hell on his self-control *and* his plan to win her back.

Hell he probably deserved.

Hell he was going to soak up as precious anyway.

Because it was Kelsey. It was him.

It was them.

And he wasn't going to waste a *them* moment.

Not ever again.

ELEVEN

Kelsey

SEBASTIAN KNEW.

She didn't know how she knew that, but the prickling between her shoulder blades that had been her constant companion since they'd walked into her parents' place told her that the jig was up.

At least with one brother.

Which meant that it was soon going to be up with the other.

Sighing, she picked up another dish and began to rinse it in the sink. Her mom had cooked, normally a treat in and of itself, but because Tanner was there, she'd also baked. And *that* was a gift from God herself.

She set the plate on the drying rack then moved to the next, scooping up a piece of pie crust from the apple crumble her mom had baked before she began rinsing.

Probably not the most sanitary, but that crust was like gold.

It couldn't go waste.

There was a reason she'd offered to do the dishes, and it

wasn't just because it was an effective way to get out from under Bas's intent stare. It also was because the leftovers became hers.

Cue evil laughter.

That crust? Hers. The spoonful of homemade ice cream Devon didn't finish? Hers. Also, eating to soothe her feelings. No way that could go wrong. Especially when it involved her mom's—

"You always did have a sweet tooth."

Kels shivered. Tan had snuck up on her just as she'd shoved the spoon in her mouth, so it took her a moment to fumble out an answer.

"Y-you shouldn't be here."

A stuttering response, and yet an absolutely perfect one for the situation.

After Wednesday, after the scene nine years before, he shouldn't be in her space.

He'd had his chance, he'd blown it, and she was done.

But then he leaned back against the doorframe, smiled his rueful smile, and her stomach did a little flip. "Dev and Bas are arguing about who the Gold should pick up in the draft, and your dad has chimed in with lots of thoughts."

Kels bit the inside of her cheek and turned back to the dishes. "I'm guessing you didn't watch much hockey while you were traveling."

A chuckle. "Not so much."

"I followed Dev's career," he continued, "Which reminds me, I haven't teased him about being the Sexiest Man of the Month or whatever his title was."

"Year," she corrected, rinsing another plate before eyeing the next. The one that was committing a crime against people who loved baked goods. Three-quarters of the slice of lemon cream her mom had also baked was just sitting innocently in the corner. Probably Becca's, since she was on a quest to lose the quote-unquote baby weight.

Meanwhile, Kelsey thought her sister-in-law had never looked more beautiful.

Also, she was going to eat that slice of pie, even if it made her sick.

"You should go do that," she said. "Dev hasn't gotten his share of sibling smack talk of late."

"Is that what I am?" Tanner's voice was closer. "A sibling?"

Typically, her impulsivity was her downfall. This case was no different. "It's all you're ever going to be," she blurted. "It's all you'll ever *let* yourself be."

Silence.

Stupid. Why had she taken the conversation there?

It had all been going, well, not exactly *fine* but now—

A fork appeared in front of her face.

"Eat the pie." Tanner reached across her and picked up the plate.

"What?"

He handed it to her. "You want it." A soft murmur. "You should have everything you want, even if people are scared they won't be able to give you all you deserve."

"People?"

"Me."

"Scared?"

Tanner speared a bite of pie and lifted it to her mouth. She hesitated, then her lips parted and the tangy-sweet hit her tongue.

"Scared," he confirmed. "Then. Now. But I've been thinking"—she snorted, and he grinned but continuing talking—"scared isn't always bad, not when scared can be a means to make a person give a shit." He touched her cheek. "And I give a shit about you, Kels. Always have."

Probably not the most romantic sentiment ever spoken, but his tone made up for it. And his eyes, too, sincerity pouring from the chocolate depths.

She swallowed, set the plate down. "I—"

"You guys done?" Bas asked, sticking his head in through the doorway. "We're starting a new Monopoly game since Tanner's home."

Kelsey groaned. "God, no. That's a horrible idea."

"You're only saying that because you thought you were going to win the last one."

"I *was* going to win it." She'd been kicking the entire family's butts.

Bas just shrugged and said, "We have to start fresh so Tanner can join."

"Oh," Tan said, eager to remove himself from the Monopoly war. And no joke, it *was* a war because her family took their board games seriously. "I—"

Bas didn't dispute further. "Hurry up with the dishes. Game's on in five."

She plunked her hands on her hips. "Bas—"

But he was gone, the stink. She frowned and picked the plate back up, shoving a huge, and not ladylike in the least, bite of pie into her mouth. "I had Park Place *and* Boardwalk," she grumbled. "Plus, a hotel."

Tan whistled. "Totally gonna win."

Kels glanced at him and couldn't hold back her smile. "Yes," she said. "I was."

He picked up a plate, started drying it. Amongst the many projects on her dad's to-do list in this fixer-upper was replacing the dishwasher that had died. But for right now, her mom had grunt work, and that meant Kels should get down to business. With a sad look at the pie, but a high five to her self-control, she dumped the rest of the slice in the trash then went back to rinsing. Tan stayed, and she washed and he dried in contented silence for a few minutes, time during which she felt her shoulders relax, the tension that had been making them ache ever since she'd learned the news of Tanner's return dissipating.

Maybe they could do this. Find a happy medium. Be friends —*just* friends—again.

"Tanner—"

"I fucked up, baby."

Baby.

She dropped the glass she'd been washing, and it hit the bottom of the sink, shattering. But she'd barely registered the sound of it break, the shards glittering in the bright lights of the kitchen. Because . . . *baby.*

His hand dropped onto her nape, and she startled.

"Careful," he murmured, sliding his fingers down her arm, slipping them around her wrist. He picked up one hand, lifting it away from the shards that she'd been absentmindedly reaching for, reeling from the contact, from his tone.

And she couldn't move.

Because the way he'd called her *baby.*

"Hey." Tan tugged, turning her so she faced him, so they were toe-to-toe, chests only a hairsbreadth apart.

"You—"

"I've spent too long running," he murmured.

"Tan—"

"I want you, Kelsey."

Her breath caught. "I—"

He kissed her.

Then Bas came into the kitchen. "Hey, the game's—"

All hell broke loose.

TWELVE

Tanner

OKAY, so he'd broken his promise not to touch her until she asked, but that was because she'd been about to cut herself.

He'd needed to do it.

Yeah, keep telling yourself that.

Frankly, it was easy to do that, the delusions of grandeur, when Kelsey's mouth was on his, her breasts pillowed against his chest, roses in his nose.

"Hey, the game's—"

Kelsey jumped, tearing her mouth from his and all but leaping back. Her hands flailed, and concerned one of them was going to land in the sink, Tanner nudged her out of the way. Which also meant that she ended up cuddled to his side, but as far as he was concerned, that was a good byproduct.

Even if Kelsey's face said she felt differently.

"I knew it!"

Bas was grinning as Devon popped his head in the doorway behind him. "Knew what?"

Tanner's gut sank, but he sucked it up. Choosing option three meant he knew this was eventually going to happen—that he'd have to lay it out there for all the Scotts, including Kels' brothers, and that they might want to kick his ass for even considering touching her.

She was worth it.

He'd figured that out earlier, too.

Tanner wasn't twenty-one years old, thinking he was a man when really, he was still a boy who didn't know his ass from a hand grenade.

He'd prove he was worth the risk. To Kelsey. And he'd tell her brothers to go fuck themselves if they had a problem with it.

In a nice way, of course.

But the point was Kelsey was his, and while the exposé al la Scotts had happened a lot sooner than he'd planned—mainly because *his* plan had included some wooing and maybe getting her to not hate him before he shared his feelings with the whole clan—this was also always going to happen.

So he had to roll with it.

"Kelsey has a thing for Tanner."

She gasped.

"Well, duh," Devon said.

"What?" Her ponytail flicked as she glanced from brother to brother. "You knew that?"

Bas rolled his eyes. "Hard to miss, Kels, when you were drooling after him every chance you got."

"I was—"

"Were, too," Tanner murmured.

Mouth agape, she stared up at him. "You knew?" she whispered, horror laced through the question.

His nod in response made her cheeks flush, and she tried to pull away. Since he liked her right where she was, he slipped an arm around her waist to keep her in place. "I knew because I had it bad, too," he said softly.

"How long?" she asked, relaxing against him.

Tanner's mouth tipped up. "Probably want to have that conversation without prying ears."

Kels jumped again, and he liked that she'd forgotten about her brothers in the room, liked that she'd leaned against him.

He just liked *her*.

Head swiveling, she glared at her brothers. "You two are horrible brothers."

"No," Bas said. "Horrible brothers would be horrified that my best friend is interested in seeing our sister."

"What?" Tanner asked.

Bas snorted. "Dude," he said. "You were as obvious as Kelsey, always asking about her, what she was doing for work, if she was seeing anyone serious."

Fuck.

He had.

His gut twisted. "Was that why you asked me to come back for the wedding?"

Sebastian sighed and rolled his eyes. "Seriously, man? I've stayed in touch with one person from high school, and that was you. Even when you were on the opposite side of the globe, we made an effort to talk," he said. "You're more than a friend. You're a brother."

"A brother who wants to see your sister."

Bas wrinkled his nose. "Well, when you put it like that, I can't condone it." A beat. "But if I think about my best friend, a man I've known my whole life, a *good* man watching out for my sister, then I can't think of anyone better."

Fuck.

Out there. Just like that.

And also the moment that Kelsey had had enough.

She shoved out of Tanner's arms, plunked her hands on her hips, and glared at each of them in turn. "First, I don't need anyone watching out for me. Second, I don't even know what the hell Tanner and I have—"

"So figure it out," Devon said, interrupting her before she went full rant.

"I—"

Dev slipped by Bas and crossed over to Tanner, toes almost touching, leaning down so his nose was mere inches away. "I'm going to say this *one* time—"

"Dev—"

They both ignored her.

"You hurt Kelsey," Dev said. "And I hurt you."

"I wouldn't expect anything less," Tanner said.

Devon straightened, a smile tugging at the corner of his lips. "But good luck trying to pin that one down. She's wily."

If they knew he'd had the chance to do it—twice—and had fucked up—twice—Tanner had the feeling that Dev wouldn't be quite so cavalier. Still, he kept that information to himself and nodded. "Thanks for the advice."

"You'll need all the help you can get."

Kels sighed loudly. "I'm right here."

"Also," Dev said, grin slipping free. "She hates when you talk about her like she's not in the room."

"I'm starting to remember that."

She huffed and turned back to the sink, picking up the shards of glass and tossing them into the trash.

"Careful," he, Bas, and Dev all said at once.

To which she shot them a glare that should have turned their dicks to popsicles.

Okay, not the best analogy, because now he was thinking about Kels sucking his cock and doing it in front of her brothers, and the last thing he wanted to be doing was popping a boner in the vicinity of her family.

Bas lifted his palms in surrender and slipped from the room. "I'll tell mom and dad that we'll be rescheduling Monopoly," he said over his shoulder.

Having dealt with his fair share of scary peeps in the NHL and not cowed by her glare in the least, Dev put one large hand on Kels's stomach and nudged her back from the sink. "Seems you have a long drive ahead of you. Probably should hit the road."

The last he said to Tanner, while looking over Kelsey's head.

Tan nodded. "I'll go say my goodbyes. Kels, you coming?"

Frosty brown eyes jumped to his face, and he was surprised when she nodded without argument. She rose on tiptoe and kissed her brother's cheek. "Bye." Then she walked out of the kitchen.

"Tan?"

He turned his gaze back to Dev, saw his friend had stuck his hand out.

"Be careful with her," Dev said when Tanner's palm met his. "She's a lot more than the tough, smart chick that shows on the surface."

"I know." And Tan kept his eyes on Devon's so Kels's brother would understand he knew exactly how precious she was. "She's it, Dev."

Dev's fingers tightened on Tanner's before letting go. "I know. Glad you finally got around to accepting it."

"You both knew?"

Dev released him. "Yeah." He started plucking up the remaining glass.

"Then, why?"

Why hadn't he said something sooner? Why hadn't they

told him to come back? Given their blessing? Hell, just done *something?*

"You weren't ready."

Quiet words. Truthful words.

Tanner acknowledged them with a nod. Then he left the kitchen and went to find his woman.

They had lost time to make up for.

THIRTEEN

Kelsey

SILENT CAR RIDES were the best.

Yes, that was sarcasm.

No, it wasn't the good version.

Sighing, she pulled her phone from her purse and plugged in the cord, cueing up her playlist. Anything to ease the pressing silence, anything to erase the knowing looks on her brothers' faces, the dawning glee on her parents' when Tanner had come up behind her and dropped a kiss to the top of her head.

She would have given anything for that at eighteen.

Nine years later, she just felt conflicted.

Tanner didn't say a word as she filled her car with the cheerful pop gloriousness, just as he hadn't said a word as he'd helped her into the car, or buckled her seat belt again.

Chivalry she shouldn't have accepted.

And yet she had.

Part of her knew it was because of what he'd said in the kitchen.

But could she trust it?

Should she?

How much of an idiot did it make her to sign up for a triple dose of potential heartbreak?

Tanner hit pause on the stereo.

"Hey!"

His lips curved, and Kels's heart skipped a beat. He had such a great smile. She remembered when they were teenagers and getting that smile pointed in her direction had been the best feeling in the world.

Even just seeing the edge of it now felt damned good.

Which was part of the problem.

Groaning, she pressed her fingers to her temples. This was the problem with her. She'd keep going in circles until she'd exhausted every potential avenue and outcome. The positive with that was she thought things through. The negative was that it took her away from living her own life.

It was safer in her own head.

But also probably why she hadn't had a boyfriend since Tan.

Crap or get off the pot, she imagined Cora telling her. And her friend would be right. She couldn't keep living like this, frozen in time. Not just with Tanner, but with every man she'd had in her life—

Fingers on her cheek startled her.

Kels realized Tanner had pulled the car over onto the shoulder. "Baby, what's wrong?"

Her life was a mess and her eyes were stinging, *that* was what was wrong.

She shook her head.

He made a noise of frustration and then the car shook as he shoved back his seat. "What—?" But she didn't get the chance to finish the sentence because the next thing she knew, her seat belt was undone, and she was in Tan's lap.

And tears.

Because she was a giant, swirling stress hurricane, her thoughts spinning in circles while the outcome seemed destined to bring devastation.

"Sweetheart," he murmured, hand cupping the back of her head, fingers stroking through her hair. "What's wrong?"

She sniffed, pushed against his hold so she could glare down at him. Her eyes were probably a puffy mess because she wasn't the type of girl who cried pretty. But dammit, how could he possibly ask her that question?

"What's *wrong?*" she growled, shoving harder against his chest. "Seriously? Fucking *seriously?*"

His eyes flashed, hands clenching on her waist. "Yes, seriously," he said quietly.

"Fine. You want to know?" she asked. "Here goes, little man. You'd better hang on to your hat. *You're* what's wrong with me," she snapped. "You. You and your walking away from me nine years ago. You leaving me on Wednesday. You pushing the ride today and then all but telling my family we were together." Kels threw her hands in the air. "You skipped over about a dozen steps, including apologizing to me for all of the crap you pulled."

"I apologized," he said.

Frustration made her back teeth ache. Well, that was probably because she was grinding them so tightly.

See? Her giant brain was useful for *something*.

And look at her go with the sarcasm, the good version this time.

Tanner shifted, drawing her focus back to the present. Namely, the fact that they were on the shoulder of a highway, rolling brown hills on either side of them, and cars whizzing by. Oh, and there was also the fact that she was still in Tan's lap.

But when she went to pull away, he held her in place again.

"I apologized," he said again. "When you called, I said I was sorry."

"Did you?" she asked, voice soft. "Or did you take the 'we were young and stupid line' I was throwing you and agree that we each took an equal share of the blame for that?" She jabbed him in the chest. "Also, this just in, you *haven't* apologized for leaving me naked and wanting on Wednesday, have you? Hmm?"

Calloused fingers wrapped around her wrist, brushing gently back and forth, back and forth.

But Tan's eyes were unfocused, as though he were reliving the conversation they'd had more than a year ago. Then his gaze snapped to hers, and regret crossed his expression. "You're right," he said. "Fuck. I'm so sorry, sweetheart. For then. For now. For being such a fucking idiot."

"Words a woman lives to hear," she joked because the words calmed that hurt inside her.

He shook his head, chocolate eyes sad. "I know I said it before, but I fucked up."

Kelsey sighed. "It's not all your fault, Tan. I—"

"No," he snapped. "You don't get to own my fuckups, Kels. *I'm* the one who ended things. *I'm* the one that stayed away. *I'm* the one who finally figured out that I can't keep my distance from you any longer, and that I want you in my life—"

"For how long?"

He froze. "What?"

"For how long?" she asked. "How long until you leave again?"

"I'm not."

She sighed again. "Tanner, your work takes you all over the world. It's just—"

"I quit."

Her jaw dropped open. *"What?"*

His face took on a mulish expression. "I'm burned out," he said. "I finished my contracts, and I'm taking a hiatus."

Hiatus. Right. And he'd fill it with her until he panicked and ran off again and left her behind, brokenhearted . . . or maybe just broken. She shifted, and this time, Tanner let her slip back into her seat.

But he turned to face her, eyes earnest. "I've seen more of the world than I ever could have dreamed of," he said. "What I want now is to be home."

"You didn't grow up here."

"But here is with you," he said. "And so that means my home is here."

Her heart was pounding, her eyes stinging again. God, how many times had she dreamed about hearing those words? The only trouble now was Tanner had hurt her enough that she didn't believe them.

She also didn't know how to tell him that.

But Tanner knew. *Of course* he did.

"I know it'll take time for you to trust me."

And with that huge understatement, he tugged his seat forward and turned on the music. Then he checked for traffic and got them back onto the freeway.

Another long, uncomfortable drive.

Her favorite.

At least this time, Taylor Swift was filling the silence.

Monday morning meant she was due at work.

The only problem was that she was sick. Miserably, horribly sick with a fever and a hacking cough. So. Much. Fun.

She texted Bas to let him know she'd come down with a bug but to stay far, far away because his wedding was in less than a week, and the last thing she needed to do was be responsible for being patient zero that took out the groom and then the bride. But just typing the message: *Sick. Stay away. Contagious.* Had taken all of her energy, and so she collapsed back on the couch wearing a nice blouse and pajama pants.

The blouse because for a brief moment, she'd thought if she could just get out of bed and get dressed, she'd feel better. The pajama pants because that notion had clearly failed.

Then she spent the next hour wallowing in her misery, trying to summon the energy to get up and shower, if only to slip back into fresh pajamas. In the end, she decided to just try and sleep it off. A shower could come later.

Therefore, the knock on the door that came as she was just dozing off was wholly unwelcome.

So, she let her eyes slide shut and ignored it.

The knock came again.

"Oh, for fuck's sake," she muttered, shoving to her feet, wavering for a minute, then stomping to the door.

Like a moron, she didn't look through the peephole.

Instead, she flung it open and—

Tanner was there.

"You look like shit," he said.

Kels rolled her eyes, but the movement made her already wavering body falter more, and she stumbled.

"Shit, sweetheart." He rushed forward and grabbed her arm to steady her.

She batted him away, almost fell backward in the process.

"Right," he said, using his foot to close the door before sweeping her up into his arms. The lock clicked a moment later, and then they were moving toward her bedroom.

Totally different walk than she'd wanted the last time he was in her apartment.

"You're burning up," he muttered. "When did you take some medicine?"

He was slipping her beneath the covers of her bed and goodness that was lovely, so lovely, in fact, that she closed her eyes and burrowed deeper. Tan brushed her hair out of her face. "Babe. Medicine?"

"Don't have any," she said, and when he cursed, added, "Instacart. Should be here in twenty."

A sigh. "Okay," he said. "But if it's not here by then, I'm going out to get some."

Great. Now he just needed to shut up so she could sleep.

"Want a cool cloth for your head?" he asked softly.

Since that sounded like nirvana, she nodded, though she instantly regretted the movement when her head spun.

"Easy, sweetheart," he murmured, brushing his fingers on her forehead. They were cold, and it was glorious enough that she leaned up slightly to prolong the contact. But then he broke the contact, telling her, "Be right back."

Eyes still closed and much more comfortable now that she was in bed, Kels let her body relax and slip toward sleep again.

But she wasn't so far gone as to not hear the conversation in the other room.

"Hey, Bas," Tan said. "No, she's really sick. Fever, chills, cough. You'd better stay away and tell Rachel to do the same. The last thing either of you needs is to be sick for your own wedding."

A pause. The sound of a faucet turning on and off.

"No," he said. "I don't think it's serious. I'll get some medicine in her, and I'm sure she'll be better in no time."

Another blip of quiet then, "Yeah, I'll call you if anything changes. Tell your mom to call off the dogs, okay? We'll try to keep this contained and not bring the plague to your wedding."

"Okay, talk to you later," Tan's voice rose in volume, and

then the cloth was on her forehead and it was the best sensation of her life. "Rest, sweetheart. I'll be here."

Kels didn't make the mistake of nodding this time, but she did let sleep take her under.

THE NEXT TWELVE hours were a blur.

She remembered Tanner waking her up briefly to take some medicine and drink some water before she passed out again.

By the time she woke up, it was dark outside her windows and she was a sweaty, shivering mess, her blankets soaked, her clothes sticking to her body. Tanner was there, helping her unbutton her blouse and change into fresh pajamas he must have gone pawing through her drawers to find.

"Not the way I'd imagined you undressing me," she rasped.

"Me neither," he agreed before tucking a blanket around her and carrying her to the couch. He disappeared for a few minutes then reappeared with a cup of soup, coaxing her to drink.

After she'd managed a few sips, he gave her more medicine and carried her back to bed.

That's when she fell in love with Tanner Pearson again.

He'd changed the sheets.

She felt like shit, but he'd made her soup and changed her sheets and—

He tucked her in, placed a fresh cold cloth on her forehead, and started to straighten, but she caught his hand. "Tanner?"

"Yes, sweetheart?"

Maybe it was the soup and sheets, or maybe the cold had just filed down her defenses enough to allow him in. Or perhaps, Kelsey was just giving in to the inevitable. She squeezed his fingers lightly.

"Will you stay?"

A squeeze back. "Not going anywhere, babe."

"No," she whispered because her throat was on fire. "Will you stay? Will you hold me?"

His face clouded, and her stomach rolled over.

"Never mind," she said quickly, slamming her eyes shut. "I shouldn't risk you getting sick any more than you already are after being stuck here with me all day."

"Not stuck," he replied, and his voice sounded funny.

Kels opened her eyes. Turned out that was because he was bending over to take off his pants, his shirt already having hit the ground.

Too bad she wasn't in any position to enjoy the view.

"You still have a fever, sweetheart," he said. "Sure you want me in bed with you?"

In bed with Tanner, let her think about that.

She must have snorted, because his gaze found hers and he smiled. "Trying not to perv on you while you're sick here, Kels. Gonna give me a break?"

"When have I ever given you a break, Tan?"

He smiled, rounding the bed to slip under the covers on the opposite side. "You've already given me too much, baby." Carefully, he slid an arm under her middle and tugged her back against his chest. His breath ruffled her hair and he *was* warm, but it was still the most comfortable she'd been in her entire life.

Especially when he pulled her just a little closer and whispered, "Sleep now, baby. I've got you."

FOURTEEN

Tanner

CONSIDERING the close proximity he'd had to plague-ridden Kelsey, Tanner had expected to wake up the following morning feeling like shit.

Instead, he woke with a beautiful woman drooling on his arm.

God, even that was cute, he realized, using his free hand to retrieve the damp cloth from the night before and wiping his arm.

Kels would probably die of embarrassment if she realized she'd left a puddle on his arm, but Tan had spent more than enough time in some pretty rough places around the world to not get all worked up over a little saliva.

He brought his fingers to her forehead, relieved to find it was much cooler than the day before.

Then he slipped carefully from the bed and walked into the bathroom.

The strangling noise from the bed had him whipping back around in alarm.

But then he saw Kels's face, saw that she wasn't choking on her own spit and hadn't managed to strangle herself in the sheet in the last ten seconds. Instead, her color was high like it had been when she'd been burning up with fever, and her eyes were on his groin.

Tan glanced down.

Whoops.

His boxer briefs weren't hiding much, and he was sporting major wood.

"Kels?"

"Mmm-hmm?" It was garbled, and not because her voice was raspy. Then she ran her tongue over her bottom lip, and Tanner just about died. Or at least nearly passed out due to a loss of blood flow.

"Eyes up here, sweetheart."

Now it wasn't tongue but teeth on that bottom lip, and Tanner clenched his hands into fists at his sides, trying to stop himself from going over there and showing her exactly what he thought of her using her teeth and tongue.

Mainly that he wanted them off her lip and on his cock.

Instead, he sucked in a breath and asked, "Feeling better?"

She nodded, sat up. "Yeah, baby."

Baby.

Fuck him.

Literally, please, God, would she let him come over there and fuck her?

"Good," he said with a nod and took a step back. A tactical retreat because he was getting very close to forgetting why he couldn't just go over and show her that he never intended to pass up another opportunity like last Wednesday. But she was sick, or at least still recovering. She needed care, not fucking.

No matter what her eyes were saying.

"I'm going to shower," he announced. Mostly to convince himself that was what he was going to do.

"Okay," she said and lay back down.

Tan stood in place for a long moment, torn between returning to bed and trying to do the right thing. He did the right thing because Kelsey deserved that much. He'd discovered the shower was through one of the two doors in Kels' bedroom. The other one led to a walk-in closet that was bigger than he had expected for a one-bedroom apartment in the city.

Not that Kels had filled it. Her wardrobe seemed to consist mostly of T-shirts and jeans, with a small collection of work clothes. Though she did seem to have an inordinate amount of Converse—one in almost every color of the rainbow—and an affinity for lacy lingerie. The latter of which he'd discovered after searching for some fresh pajamas for her in the tall dresser that took up one wall of the closet. The top three drawers contained all manners of lace, and he'd be a liar if he hadn't said he'd explored. He had. The deep purple set had been his favorite.

Now, just to convince her to wear it for him.

Forcing his thoughts from lace and the temptation of Kelsey, he picked up the tube of toothpaste. He wasn't about to snoop while she was conscious, so he just had to content himself with squirting some on his finger. It wouldn't have been the first time he'd gone without a toothbrush, but at the very least, he had toothpaste and could do a minimal job at controlling his morning breath.

Morning breath. Morning wood. Ha.

Shaking his head at himself, he unscrewed the cap, and—

The door opened.

Kels walked in.

"Morning," she murmured, brushing by him and reaching into a cupboard to hand him a packaged toothbrush, as though she just opened the door and found him in her bathroom every day.

"Morning," he repeated dumbly.

She picked up her own toothbrush and made short work of brushing her teeth, then crossed over to the shower and cranked it on. Water was barely hitting the pan before she turned and pulled a stack of towels out from a cupboard. Enough to dry a small army.

Then she tugged off her pajama top.

Now it was his turn to make a garbled sound.

Especially when her pants followed the shirt.

"Umm." Not his finest moment.

Kels rotated back to face him, raising an eyebrow as she stepped into the shower stall. "You coming?"

No, but she would be.

His boxers hit the tile.

FIFTEEN

Kelsey

HER HEART POUNDED, her brain was as hazy as when she'd been sporting the fever, and . . . she couldn't believe she was doing this again.

Couldn't believe she'd stripped down in front of Tanner, again.

That she'd risked sending another invitation over her shoulder to him.

What the hell was wrong with her?

Too impulsive by far—

The shower door opened, and suddenly Tanner was there, pressing against her spine, hot and hard . . . and *hard*.

"Hi," he whispered, lips at her ear.

"Hi, baby."

Baby. Again. Just slipped out. And yet she loved the way his arms tightened around her when she said it. But most especially, she loved the way he spun her around, nudged her a little further into the water, and then dropped to his knees.

"Um, Tan?"

"Shh."

He lifted one of her legs and tossed it over his shoulder.

She gasped, but then his mouth was on her, his tongue finding her clit with short, firm flicks. Her gasp turned into a moan and *shit*, he'd learned a few tricks over the years.

The water sluicing down her back, the heat of his mouth, the tight squeeze of his hand on her hip, her thigh, all had her spiraling higher and faster than she'd even spun in her life.

"Tan!" she exclaimed when he hit *just the right* spot.

Thankfully he didn't stop, didn't stop or shift away at her exclamation. Instead, he seemed to redouble his efforts, tongue moving quicker, finger slipping inside and pumping slowly.

Oh . . . holy . . . fuck.

"Oh God," she moaned, hips bucking, her orgasm right . . . *there*.

Pleasure exploded from her center, spreading out along her limbs, and her eyes drifted down, half-expecting to see that her body had been set on fire. But it was intact, and the sight of Tanner's head between her legs, his chocolate eyes burning up at her was the most erotic thing she'd ever seen.

"Hi," he murmured, carefully slipping her leg from his shoulder and holding her steady at her hips.

She bit her bottom lip.

He was on his feet in an instant, his mouth on hers, his tongue in her mouth. He tasted of her, and somehow that was more intoxicating than she would have expected.

Or maybe that was just Tanner and the chemistry they shared.

Eventually, he pulled back and Kels rested her head on his chest as she caught her breath, dizzy from the orgasm and the kiss and from the bug she'd had. "I think that kiss probably just got you sick."

He kissed the top of her head. "Worth it," he murmured.

"Been thinking of doing that since I first saw those teeth digging into that pretty lip of yours."

Her breath caught, her hand slid down his chest.

He snagged it, brought it back up. "Not this time."

"Tan—"

"Shh." Wrapping one arm around her waist, he used his other to reach for what turned out to be her bottle of shampoo, squeezing some on the top of her head then massing it into her roots.

Not the most efficient way to wash her hair, but probably the only time in her life that she felt cherished while doing so.

He repeated the process with conditioner then soaped her up.

All the while, he kept her in the warm water, only nudging her aside to briefly rinse the shampoo from his hair, the soap from his body. Then she was back under the stream, barely having a chance to get cold.

On the other hand, it was probably the coldest shower that Tanner had ever had.

Not that he seemed to mind, and paired with the gentle way he handled her, the soft words and sweet smiles, and if she hadn't already fallen back in love with him, that would have done it.

Or maybe it was that she'd never fallen out of love, and now she just felt safe enough to admit it.

The water turned off, a towel was wrapped snuggly around her, but when she went to step out of the shower, Tan stayed her. "I've got you, sweetheart," he said, tucking a towel around his hips.

"I can walk," she said, though her eyes were drooping, and fatigue was sweeping back over her.

"I know." His palm cupped her cheek. "But this time, let me take care of you."

Could she?

Dare she?

In the end, with the past and the present all tangled up, with her emotions and love so raw, how could she not?

Tanner carried her to bed and held her close as she drifted off to sleep.

KELSEY WOKE late in the day.

She was no longer wrapped in Tanner's arms, and when she pulled herself from beneath the covers to peek into the front of the apartment, she saw she was alone.

Alarm blipped through her, but she pushed it down.

Tanner wasn't going away.

At least not until after the wedding.

Way to go pessimistic, Kate would have said.

And Kate would be right. Kelsey loved the man. She didn't know how or why, but she knew that even when she'd hated him, she'd loved him.

Sighing, she walked to her closet and snagged her fuzziest socks and the sweatshirt she'd stolen long ago from Tan. It was raggedy, with holes all along the seams, and she wore it more for comfort now than warmth.

Hell, who was she kidding? She'd worn it for comfort back then, too.

Regardless, she tugged it over her head, slid the socks on, then went to brush her teeth even though she felt tired enough to go back to sleep again.

A virus and an orgasm.

Who knew that was the way to keep Kelsey Scott down?

But she was hungry in addition to tired, so she made her

way to the kitchen to rustle up some dinner or whatever meal she was currently awake for.

Her eyes found the clock, and it told her the time was just after four in the afternoon. So dinner, that was what she was making herself. Then maybe she'd force herself to stay up an hour or two so she wouldn't wake up in the middle of the night.

And if all her plans went well, she'd be back at work tomorrow, playing catch up because her four-day workweek had now become a two-day workweek. So focused on her rustling of the cabinets, she didn't hear the front door to the apartment open, nor the footsteps as they crossed the floor.

But she did feel the hands on her waist.

She shrieked, spinning around and elbowing, colliding hard . . .

With Tanner's jaw.

"*Fuck,*" he growled, hand coming up to cup the injured part.

"Shit," she exclaimed. "I didn't— You startled— *Shit!*" She patted his face uselessly for a few seconds before getting her head together and sprinting to her freezer for an ice pack. Swear to God, if she'd given Tan a giant bruise just in time for Bas and Rachel's wedding . . .

She hissed out a breath when she managed to get his palm away from his face.

A red welt was already rising on his jaw.

Shit.

Definitely a bruise then.

She wondered if she could pay the photographer to edit it out of the pictures. Or maybe pose him so the bruise was away from the lens.

Bas was going to kill her.

No, she corrected herself. *Rachel* was going to kill her. Bas would probably think it was hilarious that she'd bruised Tanner in the first place.

"So, you always abuse the people who take care of you?" he asked lightly.

She groaned. "I'm so, *so* sorry."

His warm hands went back to her waist, albeit slowly and from the front this time. "It was my fault, sweetheart. I shouldn't have snuck up on you like that."

"It's going to bruise."

A shrug. "Not like I haven't had one before."

"The wedding is Friday."

A brow rose. "I'm aware."

"You'll be bruised for the pictures."

His eyes danced as clarity dawned. "Well, lucky for the couple, they know a pretty good photographer who can easily make a bruise disappear."

Oh. There was that.

She bit her lip and heat replaced amusement in his expression. But he didn't kiss her as she'd half-expected. Instead, he just leaned close enough to rest his chin on the top of her head. "Were you looking for more medicine?"

"No. I feel fine. I was searching out dinner."

"How about I order a pizza instead?"

"I can cook," she started to protest.

"Show me that some other time, okay?" he murmured. "I'm guessing you're going to work tomorrow?" She nodded, and his arms went a little tighter. "So, at least take the rest of today off."

Kels hesitated before stepping out of his arms. Then she studied his face, looking deep into his eyes and hoping to figure out what the hell was going through his brain. "Why'd you come over yesterday?"

"Your brother texted me to ask if I was the reason you were sick and if you were playing hooky from work," he said.

"That's not your style, and when I called and texted, you didn't reply." A shrug. "So, I came over to make sure you were okay."

That tracked. Or was at least close enough to what she'd expected.

She supposed the bigger question was, "Why'd you stay?"

His chest expanded and contracted on a deep breath before he said, "Because I'd already left twice, and am not going to make the same mistake again."

"Oh."

"Yeah," he murmured. "Oh."

"You know, before the car ride on Saturday, I'd convinced myself that I was done with you." His jaw clenched. "Then ten seconds in your presence, and I knew it wasn't done, that I'd never been done."

Tan nodded. "I feel the same. I ran. I tried to shove it all down, but you were always there in the back of my mind." A beat. "And in my heart."

She sighed. "So, why did you leave then?"

"I had myself convinced that I could never be good enough for you," he said. "Fuck, it's still hard to believe that I'm going there with you now. And I was scared that losing you . . ." He trailed off, probably thinking that she'd be hurt if he admitted what she already knew.

"You were afraid to lose my parents, my brothers."

He looked away. "Yeah."

Okay, so she'd been thinking that, wondering on it, and the things her friends had said, and . . . all of it was so beyond dumb that she didn't hold back.

"How could you be so fucking stupid?" she snapped.

He jumped. "What?"

Maybe it was the bug she'd had—though probably it was more her impulsiveness—but she didn't have it in her to go easy on him in that moment. Not when he'd hurt them both so badly. Not when he'd stolen years from them.

"Never have I *ever* felt for another man what I felt for you at eighteen." Her finger went up even as she jerked out of his embrace. "*Never!* But you decided to be an idiot and take it upon yourself to deny us that—and don't tell me you didn't feel the same exact way, because you wouldn't have run for so long or so far if you didn't." She spun around then spun back, her finger waving as she ranted. "And you wouldn't be right back in my life the moment you did get back."

"You're right."

"And another thing," she growled. "Have I told you how fucking stupid it was for you to leave?"

She paced away then back, her irritation growing with every step. Kelsey didn't even fully grasp *why* she was upset, other than this vague notion that he denied them something they'd both wanted, and he'd done it for a long time.

"What if Bas hadn't invited you to the wedding? Huh?" She got in his face, shoved her hands against his chest, but when she went to pace away again, he kept them trapped there. "And another thing! How could you have been—"

"So stupid?"

His lips were twisting upward, as though he were valiantly fighting back a grin.

Ugh.

Even when she was furious, he was still beautiful.

"For a brilliant woman," he murmured. "Your arguments can use some work."

She opened her mouth to argue that statement—or more realistically, probably to call him stupid again—but then Tanner lowered his head and kissed her. Suddenly, there were other things on her mind aside from stupidity. Namely, how good it felt to be in his arms, his tongue rubbing against hers.

Eventually they had to do something stupid—aka breathe—and so Kels pulled away.

Tanner cupped her cheek, their lips only a hairsbreadth apart, hot, rapid breaths brushing each other's skin.

"Stupid," he murmured. "I know."

She chuckled.

"I love you."

She stiffened, reared back. *"What?"*

"Since forever," he said, hand sliding to her nape. "You know my parents," he said. "Know what they were like. They *never* told me they loved me." She sucked in a breath. She'd known they were selfish assholes, but she hadn't known they were that cruel. "Not once did I hear they were proud. And it took me a long time to understand that I'd taken that inside me, thought that it meant *I* wasn't worthy of love rather than realizing that they just weren't capable of giving it."

Her heart pounded in her chest. "How did you learn that?"

"You, babe." His fingers squeezed lightly. "Your mom. Your brothers. Your dad." Her eyes burned as he kept talking. "Do you know the first person who told me they loved me? Your mom. The first who said he was proud of me? Your dad. The first person to make me feel like I wasn't the most pathetic lost cause in the world and might actually be worth something? *You.*" The tears spilled over. "So yeah, I panicked when I realized I had all these big feelings and didn't know how to cope. I was so fucking stupid to not have talked about it with you or your parents or your brothers. Instead, I ran and kept contact to a minimum, thinking that at least if I had them and you in that limited way, even I couldn't fuck it up."

He gently wiped the tears from her cheeks.

"I was wrong. I missed—"

Kels rose on tiptoe so she could press her mouth to his. "You're here now," she said, dropping back down and taking his hand in hers. "Also, I've loved you since you helped me patch up my knee when I was eight years old."

She'd begun leading him over to the couch, but at her words, he froze. "What—?"

"Later," she murmured. "Right now, it's time for pizza."

He blinked. "Pizza?"

Kels nodded, knowing the admissions had rubbed them both raw and they needed time to process. "Pizza. Then a movie. Then you're going to hold me again while we sleep." She ticked off the orders on her fingers. "Think you can handle that, Pearson?"

"You okay?" he asked.

She nodded again.

"Then yes, I can handle it."

So they ordered a pizza—of which, Kelsey ate way more than she'd expected considering how sick she'd been just a day before.

Then they watched a movie—an older superhero one that Tanner had missed out on while in the wilderness somewhere.

Then she went to sleep with Tanner's arms around her.

It was the best rest she'd ever gotten.

SIXTEEN

Tanner

WHEN KELSEY'S alarm went off, he half-expected to have succumbed to the flu that had taken her out. But he woke with a clear head and no fever in sight, feeling more rested than . . . well, ever.

He especially liked the part where Kels rolled over and pressed a kiss to his mouth, leg slipping over his hips to get even closer. They kissed for a while, and he got a glimpse of blue lace under her pajama bottoms when he slipped his fingers between her thighs. She was so wet and hot and responsive that he almost came in his boxer briefs as he stroked her.

But then she toppled over the edge, and he got to kiss her as she found her way back down to earth.

Best morning ever.

Especially when he held her afterward and they talked about nothing for a bit, the movie, television shows she apparently needed to *educate* him on, his favorite place he'd visited. Eventually, she asked where he'd gone the previous day, and when he told her he went to get clothes from his hotel room, she shyly suggested that he get the rest of his things and stay at her place until he figured out what he was going to do apartment-wise.

Some might say too soon.

Tanner would tell them they'd waited nine years.

That was long enough.

Now, he was walking her to her office, his camera in his hand and the sun just rising over the hills in the distance.

"Text you later for lunch?" he asked.

Kels winced. "Can't. I'll have too much work, so I'll order in and eat through lunch."

"Dinner then."

"I might be really late."

He dropped a kiss to her nose. "Then we'll eat really late. Do what you need to do, sweetheart. I'll be waiting when you're done."

She nibbled at her bottom lip, and that meant he had to kiss the small hurt better, and so it was several long minutes before they came up for air and he watched her walk into the office building.

She waved from behind the glass windows, and Tan's heart squeezed.

Yeah, best morning ever.

HIS PLANS for a late dinner didn't materialize, mainly because he'd ordered takeout around nine, then jetlag had reared its ugly head, and he'd barely managed to stay up for its arrival.

He'd left it on the counter, along with plates and forks, then retreated to Kels' couch to watch a show and wait up for her.

Which had worked about zero percent.

She'd woken him up whenever she'd gotten home then left

him early that morning with a soft kiss. The wedding was that night, and she had a full day's work to get in before heading over to Rachel's.

Tanner understood, just as he understood Bas and Rachel's reasoning for a wedding on a Friday night. Their jobs were intense, projects were vast, and they wanted to make the most of their honeymoon by sandwiching it between two weekends. But thinking about not seeing Kelsey until she walked down the aisle that afternoon for the rehearsal stung. Plus, he wouldn't even be allowed to be alone with her after. The girls would all be swept away for hair and makeup while he did "guy stuff" with the male half of the Scott contingent.

Normally he liked "guy stuff." Or at least he had before it encroached on his time with his girl.

Then it sucked.

Still, he'd dealt with being apart from her for nine years, so he could deal with one more day.

In the meantime, he was going to call Tom, tell him he'd be sending him some photos to shop around for publication and that he'd take some jobs, but only so long as they were near the city.

He knew that some of the Hollywood types had big houses up in the hills around San Francisco, so if they wanted to hire him for some shoots, he was game.

His agent picked up his phone on the first ring. "Tanner," he said. "Let me guess, you've finally come to your senses?"

Tan chose not to touch that one. "I'm sending you some pictures. Shop them."

A beat then, "That's it?"

"No." Tanner sighed. "I'm at my friend Sebastian's wedding in San Francisco tonight and busy this weekend, but starting next week, if you have any inquiries for the Bay Area, I'll begin considering them."

"You're in California?" Tom asked. "How about coming to L.A.?"

"No."

"No?"

"I said the Bay Area." Tanner tried to moderate his tone. Tom was great at his job, but he was also good at steamrolling his clients into doing what he wanted them to do . . . and sometimes forgetting what *they* wanted.

But so long as Tan was explicitly clear with his agent, Tom seemed to get the message.

"No Los Angeles. Or Seattle. Or New York," he said. "Not right now, anyway. I'm not saying I'll take the jobs you offer because I need the break, but I will say that shooting in the city has reminded me of why I like photography again."

"Oh good. That's good."

"So, make some inquiries about the photos I send you, put together a job list, and I'll let you know if any of them interest me enough to pull me from my break."

"Consider it done," Tom said then hesitated. "Just to be clear. No L.A.?"

Tanner rolled his eyes and hung up the phone.

Then he grabbed his camera and headed out the door. There was an entire city to photograph, and he intended to find every nook and cranny.

SEVENTEEN

Kelsey

SHE POKED her head outside of the bride's room, made sure the coast was clear, then tiptoed down the hall. Her heels were still inside, along with the bride, Kelsey's mom, and Heather, the maid of honor.

The wedding was starting in less than an hour, but she'd gotten a text from Tanner, telling her it was urgent that she come and meet him.

Fuck. Her brother better not have gotten cold feet.

"Psst!"

Kels turned, saw the shadowy figure in the open doorway. "I swear to God, Tanner, you are asking for a matching bruise on the other side of your jaw."

He tugged her into the room and slammed the door shut.

Then had the inane thought that she was glad she hadn't put on her lipstick yet because Tanner's mouth came down on hers, and he somehow kissed her like it was the first time all over again.

Heart threatening to pound out of her chest by the time

they finally broke apart, she looked up at him curiously. "What was that for?"

"I missed you."

Now her heart skipped a beat, but she played it cool.

"Meh."

He grinned. "Meh? That's all I warrant?"

She floated closer, her breasts rubbing his chest. "I've had you around a few days now, I've over it."

Tan snorted and reached for her hair.

Kels jumped back. "Don't you dare!"

"What?"

"The wedding's in less than an hour," she exclaimed. "I barely have time to put on my lipstick, let alone fix my hair."

"An hour, you say?"

"Tanner," she warned.

His fingers brushed along the sweetheart neckline of the lilac bridesmaid dress she wore. Her previous supposition that Rachel had already purchased the dress had been right. It was also gorgeous and fit like a glove. "I like this."

"Because you can do that?"

A nod. "But also because I can do this."

This meaning slipping his hand beneath the skirt.

"Tanner," she said again. Okay, moaned. It was definitely a moan.

"I like *baby* better." His fingers slid beneath her panties. "Please, tell me these are the purple ones." He flicked up the skirt and groaned when he saw that she was indeed wearing a dark violet lace thong. "Thank you, God."

"How did . . . you know I had . . . purple underwear?" she asked, and it was punctuated with gasps as his fingers moved along her dripping pussy.

"Because I looked."

"Not now." She groaned when he circled her clit. "You knew before you looked."

"Because I looked in your underwear drawer."

She gasped.

He grinned.

"Perv."

"You like it."

If it got his fingers inside her like this, then, yes, she had to admit she liked it. Very much so. But she also had to admit that she'd come prepared for just this eventuality.

Reaching for the side zip on her dress, she slid it down, releasing her hold on the fabric so it puddled around her.

Tan had jumped back when her clothes had started falling off, probably thinking he'd broken something, so she took the chance to scoop it up and hang it on the doorknob, thus preventing the wedding photographer from having to do more work by editing out wrinkles alongside bruises.

"Baby?" he asked.

She reached into her bra and pulled out the condom she'd stashed there earlier.

Of course, she'd been planning on a coat closet or similar *post*-wedding, but this was even better. Bad bridesmaid etiquette, but she figured Rachel would understand.

She unhooked her bra.

Tanner didn't run.

She took a step closer.

He took one toward her.

She reached for the waistband of her panties.

"You're never going to let me undress you, are you?"

Kelsey burst out laughing and when Tanner's mouth hit hers, he was laughing, too. The amusement wasn't long-lasting, however, because his tongue drove in, rubbing alongside hers at the same time, his hand shoved down the dark purple lace. She was naked and he was fully clothed, and so she began unbuttoning his shirt as quickly as possible.

Not an easy task when she was holding the condom and he was still kissing her, his hands cupping her breasts.

She cried out when he rolled her nipples between his thumbs and forefingers, moaned when he broke off the kiss to suck one deeply into his mouth, forgot about his shirt altogether when his fingers slid back between her thighs.

Then it was all about his pants.

Wrestling the button open, yanking the zipper down, freeing the glorious hot length of him.

She tore open the condom with her teeth and rolled it over his cock.

"Baby," she panted, looking around frantically for any place he could take her without ruining the hairstylist's work. Table. Bad idea. Wall. No good. Well, good, but not for her hair. A counter would work or a chair or—

Tanner sank to the ground, shoving his pants down to his thighs as he went.

"I—"

He lifted up a hand. "Ride me, sweetheart."

She didn't need to be told twice. Kels dropped to her knees, straddled him, and took him inside.

"Fuck," he hissed and slowly slid deeper.

"Fuck," she agreed, bottoming out, barely able to take the hard length of him in this position. He twitched and she moaned, leaning forward to brace herself on his chest.

"That's it, baby," he said, gripping her hips and encouraging her to move.

She rocked back and forth, biting back a scream of pleasure when he tilted his pelvis so he was hitting her clit on the outside and her g-spot on the inside. So many new tricks to explore, positions to try—

But not now.

Not because there wasn't enough time—there wasn't.

Not because of her hair—there wasn't enough hairspray in the world to keep it completely unscathed.

Not because of the wedding—what wedding?

But not now because Tanner was deep inside her, his hands tracing her body, love shining in his eyes, and she knew there was no way she was going to last a long time.

"I love you, Kelsey," he said, hands reaching for her breasts again.

His words, his touch was enough.

She flew over the precipice, her orgasm crashing over her, even as Tanner thrust up into her faster and faster until he exploded with a long, low groan.

It was long minutes later that she finally came to.

"Tanner?" she asked, her face in the square of skin she managed to expose in her weak attempts to unbutton his shirt. At least she wasn't leaving makeup stains.

"Mmm?"

"How the hell am I supposed to walk down the aisle now?"

Tanner laughed and held her tight for another few minutes before they mutually decided they had to get their asses up and back to their respective bridal party rooms. Luckily there was a trash can and some tissues in this room, so they were able to clean up, then Tanner helped her back into her dress and zipped her up while she did up his buttons.

Thankfully, she'd regained feeling in her legs enough to stagger back down the hall.

"I love you," Tan murmured at the door.

"I love you, too," she murmured back.

"You okay?"

She wrapped her arms around his waist and loved that he wrapped his around her in return, but she most especially loved when he rested his chin on her head and inhaled, whispering, "Roses."

"I'm perfect, baby."

He pulled back, cupped her cheek. "Yes, you are."

"See you at the end of the aisle?"

"I'll be standing next to the groom." A flash of teeth. "Granted, he or Dev don't figure out what we were just doing." Her mouth twitched and he pressed a kiss to each corner. "Plus, I'll be there to walk you back down it when the carnage is over."

She snorted and rolled her eyes. "Really?"

"Got you to smile," he said. "Goal achieved."

Then with one more kiss, he was gone.

A moment later, she was back inside the bride's room, three women staring at her with smug expressions. Although, her mom's was laced with tears.

"Mom?" Kels hurried over. "Are you—?"

"I'm so happy that all of my babies are happy," she said and lost it completely. Kelsey and Rachel hugged her tightly, both sniffing and wiping their own eyes while Heather went for tissues.

"This is exactly why Abby is so obsessed with waterproof mascara," she muttered, shoving the box in their direction.

Eventually, they mopped up, touched up their makeup, and slipped on their heels. Just in time, too, because Kels's dad knocked at the door, told them it was game time, then escorted her mom to her seat.

"Ready?" Heather asked.

"Why'd I make this a big thing?" Rachel replied.

"Because you deserve a big thing," Kelsey said. "And Bas does, too."

"Right." Rachel nodded. "I can do this. I'm not going to puke on his shoes—"

"Oh my God," Heather said. "Do *not* tell me your pregnant."

Surprise flickered across her face. "How'd—?"

Rachel bit her lip, probably because Heather was thunderous. "You've been holding out on us! And we just had Wine Club last night, and—"

"I only found out this morning," Rachel said. "I didn't drink last night because my stomach was off. I thought it was nerves, but then I woke up feeling nauseous and took a test and . . . you can't say a word! Bas doesn't even know yet."

Heather appeared soothed. "I'm the first to know."

"Well, you *and* Kelsey."

Heather considered that. "I'll accept that."

Rachel met Kelsey's gaze and rolled her eyes. "Glad you feel that way. Now, can I trust you guys to keep this to yourselves for a few weeks until everything checks out?"

"No," Heather said. "But I promise to wait until after the wedding."

Rachel sighed. "*And* until I give you the all-clear that Bas knows."

Another considering pause. Then, "Fine."

Kelsey shook her head. "So, now that the negotiating is complete, maybe you can go marry my brother? He's probably getting a little nervous waiting at the end of the aisle by himself."

Rachel picked up her bouquet and marched to the door. "Let's do this."

EIGHTEEN

Tanner

RACHEL MADE A BEAUTIFUL BRIDE.

But Kelsey was a more stunning bridesmaid.

That was bias talking, but Tan didn't think Sebastian would fault him for thinking his sister was the most beautiful woman in the world.

He stared at her across the aisle until she caught him looking. Then he mouthed, "I love you," and got to watch the way her face softened whenever he said—or in this case, mouthed—those words. Either way, her expression was a beautiful thing and he vowed that he was going to keep that look on her face as much as humanly possible.

"You may kiss the bride," the officiate said, forcing Tanner to focus back on the ceremony.

Bas kissed his bride for a long, sweet moment before they broke apart and were announced as Mr. and Mrs. Scott.

That detail had surprised Tanner earlier during the rehearsal, Rachel being eager to change her last name, when he knew that Bas didn't give a damn. But then Bas had told him all she'd been through, and Tanner had realized that for Rachel, this was a clean start. A new life. A new family. A new name.

Yeah, he understood that.

Bas and Rachel held hands and walked down the aisle of the church, their small gathering of friends and family filling the pews. But the cheering was loud and the love in the room all-encompassing.

Tanner couldn't help himself.

He picked up the camera he'd held at his side and snapped a few shots of the receding bride and groom, of the space. He knew the photographer they hired was totally capable, but he also knew himself.

And for that reason, he also shot several dozen of Kelsey staring after her brother, huge smile on her lips, tears streaking down her cheeks.

And a few more when she glanced at him and he dropped his camera briefly to mouth, "I love you" again, capturing her face changing and knowing without a doubt that it would be his favorite photo he'd ever taken.

Then he crossed the aisle and offered her his elbow.

As they walked out of the church, he knew that someday soon, he was going to convince her to repeat the walk, only it would be in a wedding dress and with a ring on her finger.

———

THE CAKE HAD BEEN CUT, the bouquet and garter tossed, and Bas and Rachel were plastered against each other on the dance floor.

Kelsey *had* been plastered against him but was currently giving her feet a break.

Because apparently, the five-inch stilettos she was sporting weren't all that comfortable. Funny that.

But Tan kept finding these moments where he fell more in love with her.

Standing across the aisle from her.

The way she said, "Morning" when she woke in his arms.

How she'd handed him his camera then had told him to make Bas and Rachel's night by giving them "some fancy, over-priced photos from a fancy, famous photographer."

So he'd had a quick chat with the paid photographer to make sure he wouldn't be in her way or mess up her shot list, then had gotten to work.

The discarded bouquet with its ribbons drifting down over the table.

Fairy lights buried in greenery with just a glimpse of Bas and Rachel in the background, still dancing.

A discarded pair of white heels, the moon high in the sky.

Bare toes peaking beneath white lace.

Kelsey's shining brown hair, the updo having finally given way, tumbling down her back in a riot of curls.

He shifted the camera, wanting to get a shot of her profile, when he noticed she was talking to someone, her purse in one hand, her cell in the other. Her jaw was tight, shoulders stiff.

Who was—?

He dropped the lens and his heart sank.

She was talking to Tom. Or more accurately, it appeared that she was *arguing* with Tom.

"What the fuck?" he snapped, weaving his way through the tables to get to them. What the hell was his agent doing there, and why in the fuck was he talking to Kelsey? More importantly, what had he said that had upset her so much?

She put her palm up, cutting off Tom and standing.

Then she turned and hurried away.

"Kels!" he called, but either she couldn't hear him over the music, or more likely, whatever Tom had told her had royally fucked things up between them. He finally reached his agent, his wedding-crashing, now-fired agent, and grabbed the lapels of Tom's suit, shaking him roughly. "What did you tell her?" he growled. "What the fuck did you say to her?"

Tom winced and tried to push him away. "What the fuck, man?"

Tan held fast. "I asked. What the. Fuck. Did. You. Tell. Her?"

"Jesus, Tanner, get your shit together," Tom said. "I was already in the area when you'd called, so I put out some feelers. I got the normal offers." He paused. "Then I got a fucking *incredible* offer."

"Does this offer involve staying in the Bay Area?"

"Well, no," Tom said. "But I know you're going to take it because it's only three months, but it's in Antarctica and—"

"I'm not going to Antarctica."

"You love it there!"

"I'm *not* going."

"It pays—"

Tanner's hands, still locked in the lapels of Tom's suit, tightened further. "I don't think you're understanding this, Tom. I'm done with how I used to work. I want a life. A *real* life, and that means one with the woman I love. The woman who just ran off because you upset her. And *that* means you're fired."

"Tanner," Tom said. "I didn't— She was already—"

He didn't stop to hear any more of Tom's excuses. Fuck, really? Crashing a wedding, confronting his woman. What the fuck was wrong with him? Tan ran in the direction Kels had disappeared, out the side door that led to the parking lot.

She'd looked panicked.

Fuck.

He sprinted down the hall, pushed out into the cold, eyes scanning the lot for her car.

Still there.

His pulse calmed slightly.

She was still there.

But where?

He spun in a circle, trying to catch sight of her, but there was nothing.

Except . . .

He heard her cry out.

Shit, he'd made her cry. He'd hurt her again.

Tanner ran in the direction of the sound, turning the corner and going from panicked, worried, and slightly pissed-off to enraged.

Some idiot had his hands on her.

"Stop," Kelsey said, trying to shove him off and teetering on her heels.

The man gripped her hips, one hand snaking down to grab her ass. "I just want a little—"

Tanner stopped thinking. He reacted, ripping the man off her and punching him hard in the face. Pain erupted in his hand, but he didn't stop, just kept at him with his fists until he felt Kelsey's palm on his back.

"Tan. Stop."

Fuck.

He dropped the drunk, who was sporting a bloody nose and already forming a black eye and turned to her.

"I'm not going to Antarctica."

Her face changed, concern morphing into confusion. "Um, I know that, Tan."

"But Tom said he'd told you I was leaving."

She pulled out a tissue from her purse and wrapped it over his fingers. At the same time, a burly dude in an apron burst out of the restaurant. "I saw the whole thing, got it on video, too.

Cops are coming." His eyes went to Kelsey. "Sorry, I couldn't get out here in time to help. That guy is a fucking problem."

Kels sucked in a breath and Tanner saw her hands were shaking, even though she forced her words to sound light. "Luckily, I'm friends with Rebecca Darden. I think she'll be able to make him go away for a long time."

The fucker on the ground actually whimpered then started to push to his feet, as though he were going to run.

Thankfully, the chef stomped a foot on the man's chest and held him in place. "Got him," he said. "I'm Brent, by the way."

"Tanner," he replied.

"Kelsey," she said.

"I know, darlin'," Brent said, "I've seen you in here with your friends. But I think you'd better go sit down now."

She nodded, and Tanner slipped a hand around her waist, noticing that she'd gone from hands shaking to full-body trembling. "I'm taking her to the back. We'll be there if the cops need us to make a statement."

"Roger that," Brent said, and Tanner bustled Kelsey to the back room. The tables were decorated for the wedding, the remnants of a buffet along one wall, but thankfully most of the wedding party was out back on the covered patio, socializing and dancing.

He'd thought a bar was an odd place for a wedding, especially since everyone had been bustled out to the patio for dessert and dancing after finishing their meals, but now Tan was just glad to have a warm, empty room to bring Kels.

"I wasn't paying attention," she murmured as he sat her down on a chair and squatted in front of her. "I should have been paying attention—"

"That was *not* your fault," he said.

She blinked.

"No one has the right to touch you without you wanting them to. Got me?"

Hard words. Sharp words. But they seemed to snap her out of her trembling.

"Thank you," she said. "For being there. I couldn't get him off me a-and I was getting really scared."

Tanner wrapped his arms around her, holding her tightly against his chest, brushing his hand through her hair. "I'm not going anywhere, sweetheart."

"I know." He opened his mouth to tell her again that Tom was wrong, but then she shifted back, glancing down at his knuckles. "Still bleeding," she murmured, pulling back the soaked tissue.

"It's nothing."

"You came." She smiled up at him. "I knew you would come. That you weren't leaving."

"But you ran off, sweetheart."

Her face changed from hazy to focused and alarmed. "I need my phone."

"What?"

"Tanner," she said. "I need my phone. It's why I was out there. Why—" When he held it up from where he'd retrieved it and her purse from the ground, she snatched it from his hand and immediately began dialing.

"Hello? Mark? Yes, I'm okay." She sucked in a breath. "No, you have to reset the program, and . . ." She rattled on for several minutes in a language he didn't understand. "No. Not like that. It'll crash the whole system. You need to . . ." She kept talking, and Tanner finally began putting the pieces together. By the time she hung up after a, "Yes, exactly that. Now there shouldn't be any further problems, but call me if something comes up," he understood.

She set her phone on the table, still pale, but no longer shaking or out of it.

"You didn't leave because of Tom."

Kels shook her head, lips curving up. "I have my intern watching the new program we're testing this weekend." She shrugged. "He fucked up. Thankfully, it was salvageable."

"You didn't leave because he told you—"

Her finger pressed to his lips. "I didn't leave because of him or even because of you. If you'd checked your phone, you would have seen I texted you I was out front."

"But—"

"Also, I'm not a woman who changes her mind easily. So, when I told you I loved you, I meant it, and I'm not letting that go this time." Her finger lifted. "I should have fought harder last time, but then again"—her voice softened—"I think we both have a lot of should haves."

He touched her cheek. "Yes, we do."

"And I also understand why you left before. I mean, I think it was really fucking stupid, but you were also twenty-one," she teased. He snorted, but his lips were curving.

"Thanks for that," he muttered. "And for the record, I told Tom I would only take jobs in the Bay Area for now."

Her eyes went soft. "Baby."

"I want us to have a chance to get back to what we had, to build something strong."

"I don't care if you take the job in Antarctica. Or one in Australia. Or Timbuktu. I don't care because I know you'll come back, Tanner." Her forehead dropped to his. "And that is all I've ever needed."

"I love you."

More soft that Tanner soaked up and held tight.

"Also, I fired Tom."

"If it was because of what he said to me, that's stupid. If it's because he crashed my brother's wedding, then maybe he deserves it." Lips brushing across his. "But also, maybe I can help him learn some appropriate boundaries before you shitcan him."

"I don't think that's possible."

"I'm always up for a challenge." A beat. "But if he crashes *our* wedding, then he's definitely fired."

He laughed and kissed her gently, putting every bit of emotion and love into the contact, knowing that he was the luckiest man on the planet to somehow have found his way back into Kels's life.

"You do a lot of nude shoots, huh?" she asked as she pulled back.

"I'm going to kill Tom."

But he didn't get a chance because right then the police showed up.

NINETEEN

SHE WAS WAITING on the beach, toes in the sand, as Tanner picked his way through some tide pools several hundred feet away when suddenly he straightened and gestured for her to come and come quick.

Heart skipping a beat, she jumped to her feet and ran over.

Was there something wrong? Or was there something really cool?

She couldn't tell from his expression.

But then she got close enough to see and immediately relaxed. Not wrong, something in the cool column.

"Look," he murmured, dropping his lens and pointing slowly to the small pool of water.

"*Oh*." Her breath caught as the cutest little hermit crab poked his head out of his shell. Long spindly legs, a pair of tiny eyes, and good lord, adorable little skittering as it made its way across the rocky bottom.

"He's so cute."

A tug of her ponytail. "How sexist to presume it's a boy crab."

Since he was right, she chose not to acknowledge him.

"Either way, it *is* cute. But I wasn't calling you over for that."

"Okaay." Her heart skipped another beat, and she fought the urge to bite her bottom lip. She'd been thinking a proposal was coming. Okay, well she'd snooped and found a ring, but it wasn't her fault he'd hid it in his T-shirt drawer. She liked to wear his shirts to sleep in. Still, with the waves crashing and the sun setting behind them, this would be the absolute *perfect* place for a proposal.

Tan pointed down again. "I think he or she is the answer to your delivery problem. Look how it maneuvers easily across the uneven surface."

Disappointment slid through her even as she watched the crab move and processed what he was saying. "Holy shit, Tan. You're right! If I could get engineering to model the legs after something more like this, we could study the movement and build in some of the better adaptations. This could really help—"

She glanced over, but he wasn't crouched next to her anymore. And when she spun to find him, her breath stuttered to a stop in her lungs, she found him down on one knee, camera in one hand, a ring in the other.

"Tanner?"

He lifted the camera, and she heard the click of the shutter. "Baby," he murmured, letting it hang from the strap around his neck, and reaching for her hand. "I love you more than life. I know that we're new and all, but will you—"

"Yes!"

Cue her impulsivity ruining whatever speech he had planned. But Kelsey didn't need it. She knew he loved her, knew they were meant to spend the rest of their lives together. She didn't need more words.

She just needed Tanner.

He grinned, nonplussed that she'd probably ruined a moment he'd been planning for a while, and slipped the ring on her finger. Then they were both on their feet and his mouth was on hers, the camera pressed between them.

Before she could adjust it, a wave slammed into them—well, mostly into Tanner's back—and later, when she saw the pictures, Kels was thrilled the precious piece of equipment had been safely stowed between them.

Her hair over one shoulder as she'd studied the crab.

Her surprised face when she'd seen him on one knee.

The love in her eyes when she'd said his name.

He'd captured them all.

Just as easily as he'd captured her eight-year-old heart with a Band-Aid and an ice pack.

Just as surely as he held her heart now.

And Kels knew she'd never want it any other way.

EPILOGUE

Trix

SHE WATCHED HER FRIEND, Tanner, kiss his fiancée again, then checked her watch, wondering two things.

First, why she'd come back to California in the first place.

And second, what the hell kind of drugs she'd been on when agreeing to this date in the first place.

The only good thing about it was that she had buffers. Tanner and his fiancée. Heather, her half-sister and the only decent member of her family, along with Heather's husband, Clay, who was pretty to look at and not too annoying. For a man.

Probably not the best attitude to have going into a blind date, but she'd shown up, hadn't she?

Anyway, the dinner had also meant she'd been able to see Tanner. She'd met the photographer in sub-Saharan Africa almost five years before while she'd been working and he'd been documenting the health crisis for the Red Cross. They'd kept in touch, and he'd invited her to his wedding. It had been a surprise to both of them that they each knew Heather.

But that was the way the O'Keiths worked.

Invading their way into everyone's lives.

Even if they didn't want it.

Regardless, she was back in California for the time being, ready to begin a new chapter in her life.

Apparently, that meant starting by dating.

At least that was Heather logic.

Or maybe her own brand of stupid.

Whatever it was that had convinced her to come, she was there now and was going to make the best of it. Or at least that *was* her thought until she recognized who was approaching the table.

Him.

Trix slammed her eyes closed and counted to five.

It could not be him.

Could not—

She opened her eyes.

Clay was on his feet, shaking the man's hand, shaking *Jet's* hand, and making introductions all around. Heather looked thrilled, probably because Jet was gorgeous and funny and smart—

"And this is Heather's sister, Trix. She's a nurse."

Jet knew that.

Because he knew her. *Intimately.*

The doctor and the nurse. So cliché. So stupid on her part to think that things in her life might have turned out differently.

He'd been smiling as he turned to meet her, and it was almost comical to see his expression darken to fury. Or it *would* have, if that fury hadn't been directed at her. By then his hand was in hers, mid-shake and *fuck* if his touch didn't still make sparks shoot down her arm.

She went to pull back, but he held fast then jerked her forward, as though he were giving her a hug in greeting.

No one at the table could see that he was hissing in her ear.

"What the fuck are you playing at, Trixie?"

She did some hissing of your own. "*Nothing.* I had no idea this date was you because I sure as hell wouldn't have come," she snapped, ignoring the way his scent coiled in her stomach, sending little tendrils of heat down between her thighs. "You're the last person I'd want to see at this table. And that includes my parents or maybe even Hitler, you freaking asshole."

"Trixie," he began.

"Fuck off, Jet," she said then pulled back and plunked into her chair, not about to ruin everyone's night just because she couldn't stand the man she'd been set up with.

She'd endure.

It was what she did.

Jet sat down next to her, and she tried to force herself *not* to look.

She didn't succeed.

And what she saw on his face wasn't fury, not any longer. It was confusion and hesitation.

Good. After what he'd done to her, she deserved a man treading around her with a bit of hesitation. She'd been hurt before—heartsick and sad, a few times even devastated—when her relationships had ended.

But Jet had broken her.

He was the *one* man she'd let in, who she'd shared her baggage and hopes, her pain and desires. Then he'd shown about as much care with her exposed and vulnerable heart as a physician tossing a soiled bandage onto the floor.

For a nurse to pick up.

Because that was all she'd ever been to him.

A convenient place to stash his dick before he'd tossed her aside, dirty and used, and she had to cobble herself together enough to throw away those pathetic hopes she'd been hanging on to.

"Trixie," he murmured.

She smiled brightly and picked up the menu. "I've heard the prickly pear margaritas are delicious," she announced to the table at large.

As she knew it would, that turned the conversation to Kelsey, who began bantering with the table at large, and pretty soon, the waiter came over to take their orders.

All through dinner, she managed to keep the conversation light, to keep her physical and verbal distance from Jet while still pretending to get to know him enough to satisfy the others at the table.

Her fatal flaw began when she slipped away to use the bathroom.

Because when she came out, Jet was standing in the hall.

Sniffing, she started to move past him.

His hand on her arm stilled her.

"What Jet?" she snapped. "What could you possibly have to say to me?"

A growl. "Nothing."

"Good."

"*Everything*."

He kissed her, and the world went topsy turvy.

BAD BLIND DATE

COMING APRIL 19TH, 2020

Preorder Trix and Jet's story here.

BILLIONAIRE'S CLUB

Did you miss any of the other Billionaire's Club books? Check out excerpts from the series below or find the full series at www.amazon.com/gp/product/B07JVRRGCT

Bad Night Stand
Book One
www.books2read.com/BadNightStand

Abby

"I'M THE BEST FRIEND," I said and lifted my chin, forcing my words to be matter-of-fact. I'd been through this before. "You might be fuckable to the nth degree and perfect for Seraphina, but I refuse to set her up with a liar."

In a movement too quick for my brain to process, my stool was shoved to the side and I was pinned against the bar, heavy hips pressing into me, a hard chest two inches from my mouth.

Seraphina whipped around at the movement and I could just see her over Jordan's shoulder, her blue eyes concerned.

"Hi, Seraphina, I'm Jordan," he said, calm as can be, gaze locked onto my face then my eyes when mine invariably couldn't stay away. "I'm going to borrow your friend for a minute."

"Abs?" she asked, and I knew she'd go to bat for me right then and there if I needed her to.

"Weasel or no?" I managed to gasp out. For some reason, I couldn't catch my breath.

Not that it had anything to do with Jordan.

No, it had *everything* to do with him.

"Weasel?" he asked.

I shook my head, focused on my best friend. Weasel was our code name for the men trying to weasel, quite literally, their way into my pants and then into hers.

I was just about ready to say fuck it—or me, rather—even if Jordan was a Weasel. He smelled amazing. His body was hard and hot against mine.

And it had been way too long since I'd had sex.

"No chemistry on my part—" Seraphina began.

"Your friend isn't who I'm attracted to," Jordan growled out. "You are, and it's fucking pissing me off that you don't believe that."

Bad Breakup
Book Two
www.books2read.com/BadBreakup

CeCe

"You're even more beautiful than I remember," he said, and the rough edges of his accent hacked at the words, making them more of a growl rather than a soft sentiment.

Her breath caught, and she found her eyes drawn to the stormy blue of Colin's.

And she stared again, utterly entranced before she remembered how it had all ended.

Her in a white dress.

Alone, except for the priest who'd given her a pitying look and invited her to stay as long as she needed.

But it had always been like this, Colin's gruff words winning her over. They were unexpected from him—he was typically so reserved and taciturn. And that compliment, freely given as it was, chipped away at any defenses she managed to erect.

The problem was that his words weren't always followed up by action. In fact, they were typically trailed by pain for her and fury for him.

The hurt of those memories—of Colin so angry, her so broken—helped shore up her resolve.

"Don't say things like that," she snapped and started to pop her earbuds back in. Her friends at home had filled her phone with a slew of romantic audiobooks and she decided that she much preferred fictional heroes at the moment.

At least if they broke their heroine's heart, it was only once.

Colin had already broken hers twice.

She wasn't looking for a round three.

—Get your copy at www.books2read.com/BadBreakup.

Bad Husband

Book Three
www.books2read.com/BadHusband

Heather

"I'm getting drunk," he said, but allowed her to pull him inside the car so that her driver could shut the door behind them.

"You're already drunk," she said.

He stiffened. "*More* drunk."

"Fine," she said, half-worried he was going to launch himself from the sedan. She'd never seen Clay like this. Usually he was so cold and uncompromising, impenetrable even under the toughest of negotiations. He was . . . well, he was typically as *Steele*-like as his last name decreed.

She wrapped her arm through his in order to prevent any unplanned exits from the vehicle and gave the driver the name of her favorite bar. "If you really want to drink, let's do it right."

And *then* she'd drop him at his hotel.

Except it didn't happen that way.

Yes, they hit the bar.

Yes, they drank.

Yes, they got plastered.

But then they woke up . . . or at least, *Heather* woke up.

Naked.

With a softly snoring Clay Steele passed out next to her in bed.

That wasn't the worst part.

Because Heather woke up naked and with a softly snoring Clay Steele in her bed *and* she was wearing a giant diamond ring on her left hand.

Still not the worst part.

That came in the form of a slightly crumpled marriage certificate tucked under her right cheek.

And not the one on her face.

She pulled it from beneath her, a cold sweat breaking out on her body, dread in every nerve and cell.

She *still* wasn't prepared for the horror she found.

The marriage license had been signed by . . . Heather O'Keith and Clay Steele.

Holy fuck, what had she done?

—Get your copy at www.books2read.com/BadHusband.

Bad Hookup
Book Four
www.books2read.com/BadHookup

Rachel

The man didn't take the hint. He didn't leave.

Why won't he leave?

She dropped her chin to her chest.

"So," he finally said after another lengthy—and silent—moment. "Gay, taken, or not interested?"

"Oh my God," she moaned, one hand coming up to push her bangs off her forehead. "This is *not* happening."

"I—" A beat then his voice was incredulous. "I *know* that moan." Warm fingers grasped her wrist, tugged until she could see him in all his yumminess.

Her moment of weakness. Her hookup because she'd been feeling desperate and lonely and—

"It's you," he said softly.

Yes, it was *her*. Rachel, the good girl who didn't sleep around, who *certainly* didn't hook up with random strangers in a bar.

Rachel, who *had* hooked up with a stranger.

The sex had been damned good. Incredible, actually.

But it had been just that. Sex. And she hadn't been able to let go of the guilt. She'd now slept with a grand total of two men in her life, and one of them was her husband.

"I—" She tugged at her wrist. "I need to go."

—Get your copy at books2read.com/BadHookup.

Bad Divorce
Book Five
www.books2read.com/BadDivorce

Bec

Bec really didn't expect to see another person waiting for her when the doors opened with a soft *ding* and she stepped off.

But there *was* another person waiting just outside her front door.

A person she never expected to see again.

Luke Pearson.

Her ex-husband.

It was one-fucking-thirty in the morning, and her ex-husband was sitting on the floor outside her apartment.

Asleep.

Fuming, she marched over to him and kicked his shoe. Hard.

"Luke. Why in the ever loving fuck are you here?"

His lids peeled back and sleepy green eyes met hers. "Becky," he murmured. "You're gorgeous as always." The drowsiness began to fade from his expression. "Did you just come from work?" He glanced down at his phone. "Do you know what time it is?"

"Of course I know what time it is—" Bec bit back the words. Fuck, but wasn't this conversation an exact replica of the broken record one they'd had *way* too many times over the course of their relationship?

She crossed her arms. "Never mind that." A glare that had withered balls much bigger than Luke's "Why did you break into my apartment?"

He stood. "First, I didn't break into your apartment. This is the hall. Second," he hurried to say when she opened her mouth to argue semantics, "I didn't break in. You used our anniversary as the code."

Oh for fuck's sake.

Well, she was changing that tomorrow . . . today . . . fuck, *yesterday*, now that—

"Go away, Luke," she said, pushing past him and unlocking her door while blocking his view of the keypad that was identical to that of the elevator. Her front door's code was not the date of her anniversary with her ex.

But Luke probably already knew that, given that he had been sitting on the floor of her hallway rather than on her couch, beer in hand, feet making prints on her glass coffee table.

Men.

Fucking men.

She slammed the door closed behind her and threw the dead bolt. The knock approximately one second later did not surprise her. Bec dropped her briefcase to the floor then opened it just enough to shoot angry eyes at him through the narrow gap the dead bolt allowed.

Serious green eyes fixed onto hers. "We need to talk."

"Luke," she snapped. "I'm exhausted. It's the middle of the

night. I wouldn't have any patience to talk to my best friends right now, let alone my ex-husband."

"Funny story about that," he said, his lips curving. "Turns out that I'm not actually your *ex*-husband."

—Get your copy at www.books2read.com/BadDivorce

Bad Fiancé
Book Six
www.books2read.com/BadFiance

Seraphina

Sera was alone, pining after a man who'd created the latest social media craze.

Yup. Her life was *ah-maz-ing*.

Tate cleared his throat, and Sera realized she'd been staring at him dumbfounded for a good couple of minutes.

"How can I help you today?" she asked. "I do hope"—*Do hope?* What was she, British? *Ugh.*—"I-uh . . . I hope you were able to find a house. The agents I passed along are very good at finding unique properties, and I even gave them a few locations to start with . . . " She bit her lip, attempting to stop the ramble.

"No."

Just no.

Um. Okay.

He lifted a hand, rubbed the back of his neck. The movement made his shirt lift, exposing several inches of flat stomach and tan skin and, oh God, a trail of blond hair leading south. Her mouth watered, desperate to trace that path with her tongue—

Sera sucked in a breath, popped to her feet.

"Ah. I'm sorry." She picked up a random file, pretending to know what was in it. "I'm actually really busy, so this will have to continue another time."

Like never.

She rounded her desk, forced a smile. "Mr. Conner," she said when he didn't move. "I'll have my assistant schedule something soon."

"Seraphina."

She shivered at the sound of her name on his lips—soft, a little raspy, and deep enough to conjure all sorts of unhelpful fantasies in her mind.

Shaking herself, she moved to open the door.

Suddenly, Tate was there, hand on hers, body inches away, spicy scent inundating her senses.

Sera's breath caught. "What are you—?"

He seemed to be arguing with himself then finally, those piercing blue eyes locked onto hers. "I need you to marry me."

—Get your copy at www.books2read.com/BadFiance

ALSO BY ELISE FABER

Breakout

Checked (March 29th, 2020)

Chauvinist Stories

Bitch (Feb 16th, 2020)

Cougar (March 1st, 2020)

Whore (March 15th, 2020)

Life Sucks Series (all stand alone)

Train Wreck

Phoenix Series (read in order)

Phoenix Rising

Dark Phoenix

Phoenix Freed

Phoenix: LexTal Chronicles (rereleasing soon, stand alone, Phoenix world)

From Ashes

KTS Series

Fire and Ice (Hurt Anthology, stand alone)

ABOUT THE AUTHOR

USA Today bestselling author, Elise Faber, loves chocolate, Star Wars, Harry Potter, and hockey (the order depending on the day and how well her team -- the Sharks! -- are playing). She and her husband also play as much hockey as they can squeeze into their schedules, so much so that their typical date night is spent on the ice. Elise is the mom to two exuberant boys and lives in Northern California. Connect with her in her Facebook group, the Fabinators or find more information about her books at www.elisefaber.com.

facebook.com/elisefaberauthor

amazon.com/author/elisefaber

bookbub.com/profile/elise-faber

instagram.com/elisefaber

goodreads.com/elisefaber

pinterest.com/elisefaberwrite